FOG BANK

The Complete Story

By Leigh McQueen

COPYRIGHT NOTICE

© 2015 by Leigh McQueen (original story)
© 2016 by Leigh McQueen (Compilation)
River Oaks Press
All Rights Reserved

This is a work of fiction. All aspects of the story are a product of the author's imagination and any resemblance to persons living or dead is purely coincidental. This book is licensed and may not be resold or given away. The reproduction, resale, or distribution of this book in whole or part, by electronic or any other means, without the written permission of the author or publisher, is unlawful piracy and is punishable by law. Support of the author's rights is deeply appreciated.

ISBN-13: 978-1535350112

ISBN-10: 1535350113

http://leighmcqueen.com

This is dedicated to my husband, Keith, who read, re-read, and re-read again each draft of this first story and he never got tired of it. That act showed more love and support than words could say.

FOG BANK

Just before sunset, the Fog Bank rolled into the big city like a ghost train. Cities and their populaces were normally avoided. No need to risk being seen by the humans. However, there was a Siren in this city. The Fog rolled in and waited. This one did not know she was a transmitter of pain and need, mixed with an odd strength – an irresistible combination.

The Fog gathered itself into swirling grey/black coils.

It pulsed with need as it waited in the shadow of a copse of trees several yards from the Siren's back door. It was a patient being, but it had strong appetites and would not wait forever. In the shadows, it flexed its power and then grew still.

The moment rapidly neared when it would first introduce itself to the Siren and get a taste of what it needed – and she would get a taste of what *she* needed.

Sunset was near and so was the Siren. The Fog waited.

******

Eva was self-conscious every time she saw her home through someone else's eyes. She watched Stanley's face as he slowly took in her bookshelf-lined living room, and she could see that his opinion of her as a freak was permanently fired in the kiln of his observation.

Soft light filled her living room from several strategically placed lamps. As Stanley's eyes moved along, she watched him read the titles tattooed on the spine of each tome. They were lined up in an endless parade to create the great walls of imagination that protected her from the outside world. Her face grew hot with embarrassment.

"You must *really* be a fan of vampire novels." Stanley had stopped reading the many titles. He turned his silver-eyed gaze toward her after he took in her collection of every one of Charlaine Harris' Sookie Stackhouse novels, as well as Stephen King's *Salem's Lot*, Bram Stoker's *Dracula*, Laurell K. Hamilton's books, Anne Rice's work, and Stephenie Meyer's *Twilight* series of books. Eva had every book in both hardback and paperback, if both were available. Good thing he had not gotten his hands on her Kindle. She kept digital copies, as well.

She tried to laugh it off. "It's a guilty pleasure."

Stanley laughed companionably, but she could see the nervous energy in his face. *He wants to bolt from here. He's laughing as if he understands, but he really doesn't.* It was evident in his eyes. He looked at Eva as if assessing whether or not she carried a weapon.

She sighed. She could not change his opinion. He would believe what he wanted to believe. It shouldn't matter what he thought about her, but she knew it did. It mattered. They had been co-workers for five years and he had been her supervisor for the last two years. They had been friends too, sort of.

She turned to the closest shelf and selected Stephenie Meyer's *Eclipse*. She handed it to him and he accepted it warily as if he thought she would do something unexpected.

"Here's *Eclipse*. I hope your girlfriend enjoys it. I know what it's like to get addicted to a series of books and not be able to get the next book right away. It will make you crazy."

"Yeah, I think she will be really excited when I give this to her. I'll return it as soon as she's finished," he said. "Shannon is a fast reader. You probably will have it back by next week."

"Whenever. I'm not worried about it." She actually *was* worried about it, but she tried to act casual. She did not loan out her precious books very often. "See you at work tomorrow?"

"Yes, I'll be there. TGIF, right? Got any big plans for the weekend?" Even as he asked the question, Stanley had already turned. He hurried toward the front door.

"No, no big plans. I might have a date, but that's still up in the air."

Stanley stopped in his tracks. "A date? Really?"

"Yes. A date. Is it really so hard to believe?" Eva clenched her fists. She could tell tears were imminent. She needed Stanley to go away. She hated that his opinion mattered so much. She had always felt something for him. She never put a label on it, and it was normally under control, but now it reared its head. *Why couldn't he ever have noticed me? Am I really that lackluster?*

"No, I only meant that I didn't know. Since you and Bart broke up, you're so quiet and private. You seem to prefer solitude."

Eva fought back the sarcastic retort she had been about to hurl toward him like a spear. She managed to stop herself from her knee-jerk response. Barely. She knew it would have been childish and petulant.

Stanley did not deserve that. He hadn't meant any harm. Instead, she simply said, "You assumed wrong. I do not prefer solitude."

While she fought her temper tantrum, Stanley didn't wait for her to open the front door for him. He rushed outside and down the front steps, calling to her from over his shoulder, "See you later, Eva. Sorry about the stupid comment."

She waved at his back, then closed and bolted the door. She leaned against the door and endured a clench of emotion that set up in her chest. *What is this about? I thought you were over your cute little crush on the boss? Get a grip, Eva.*

Her cat glided up and wound his way around her ankles. Chester's purring seemed monstrously loud in the quiet entry hall. His warm body contrasted with the cool tile of the dark entryway. His affection eased the knot that threatened to slip up from her chest and choke her. She spent several moments listening to Chester's purring, which held the silence of her modest house at bay.

"What would I do without you, Chester?" She picked up the huge, gray cat and nuzzled him. He purred and rubbed his face against her cheek, then jumped down from her arms. She sighed. "Well, I guess a little love is better than none at all. You want some dinner?"

Chester wandered over to the French doors that occupied the area between her kitchen and living room. The lovely doors were the reason she bought the little house. They led out onto a small patio area and overlooked the yard.

Chester stared fixedly outside. Daylight had faded, but there was still a pastel painted twilight. She noticed one of the plants she kept on the back patio was turned over.

She opened one of the doors to go outside and set the plant right. Luckily, only a miniscule amount of soil had spilled. She dusted off her hands after quickly fixing the situation.

She noticed Chester waited in the open doorway to the house. Normally, he would have come outside and sniffed around the patio. She followed the direction of his stare to a wooded area at the edge of her property.

There was a bank of patchy fog there. She watched it for a moment. The hairs on the back of her neck bristled. After a long moment, she dismissed the anomaly and went back inside. Once she shut the door, she glanced back at the barely visible patch of fog and flipped the deadbolt.

She walked back to the living room and switched on the television and tuned in to the local news. Whenever she was home, it was her habit to keep the television on. Sometimes, the TV remained on throughout the night. She understood the psychology of this practice, but she was not entirely comfortable with the conclusion she would have to draw regarding herself if she examined it too closely. She listened to her favorite anchorman, Charles Kellerman. After living on her own for the past five years, Charles Kellerman had become like family to her. She loved the way he ended his broadcast each evening – "From our family to yours, good evening."

"Good evening, Charles," Eva said as she walked into the kitchen area. She opened the refrigerator. She decided on an Italian inspired chicken dish she often enjoyed. She sported a wicked grin as she poured herself a glass of moscato. Her conservative mother would never approve.

"Oh, well, what Mama doesn't know--" She giggled as she took a sip. Her phone rang and she nearly dropped her glass. Her startled reaction caused her to splash some wine onto the counter. "Shit!"

She looked at her caller ID and was not at all surprised to see it was her mother calling. She picked up the phone. "Hi, Mom."

"Eva? Is that you? Well, I can call off the search now. I have been so worried. I haven't heard from you in three days! What is going on?"

Eva sighed and looked around the kitchen for a clean dishtowel to wipe up the spilled wine. "Nothing is wrong, Mama. I've just had an extremely busy week at work."

"Well, you could have called. Do you know how worried I get? And, I get lonely. I know you are lonely, too. We both are.

"All we have is each other, Eva, and you went and moved to the big city. What kind of daughter does that to her poor, lonely mother?"

That was five years ago. I took a job in Nashville to get away from your smothering ways. She allowed herself a small smile as she thought of the response she wished she could give, but knew she never would. She held the phone away from her ear and the tinny voice in the phone went on in the same fashion for another 20 minutes.

She put the phone on speaker and listened as she moved about the kitchen preparing a tasty dinner for one. Finally, when her mother had no more bitter venom left, she bid Eva a good night and told her how much she loved her.

"Yeah, Mom -- love you, too," Eva said, as she ended the call. She carried her plate and wine glass toward the living room.

A sound drew her attention to the patio. The same plant was knocked over again.

"What the hell?" She put her plate and wine glass back on the kitchen counter. She unlocked the doors and stepped outside to fix the plant again. She examined the pot. It was a wide, round terra cotta pot. It was heavy, with a low center of gravity. It should not tip easily.

As she righted the potted plant, she looked back to see Chester staring again. She refused to look. Like someone whistling in a graveyard, she ignored her goose bumps and quickly finished the job. Once inside, she locked the doors again.

Gathering her plate and wine glass again, she carried the feast to the coffee table in her living room. She fired up her laptop computer and browsed on Facebook as she ate her dinner, but not before she took a picture of her latest cooking triumph.

She posted, "Tuscan chicken a la Eva! YUM!" She had five "likes" within 30 minutes of posting. That was impressive as she only had about 120 friends, and more than half were strangers.

As her second glass of wine made her feel sentimental, Eva indulged in her favorite pastime and stalked her ex-boyfriend's Facebook page to stare at the latest pictures of his new, bikini-clad girlfriend.

Her tanning bed complexion and firm body only made Eva hate her more. (That, and the fact that she spelled her name "Kimberli" with an "i." Eva thought the white trash spelling made the name seem grammatically incomplete.)

Kimberli was a decade younger than Eva and a decade and a half younger than Bart, Eva's ex. More reason for hating, as far as she was concerned. Eva and Bart dated for over five years. He kept telling her he needed more time before settling down. Now, she stared at the engagement pictures on Kimberli's page – at least what pictures she could view without actually becoming "friends." There were several close up shots of the most gorgeous ring Eva had ever seen. Eva wanted to puke.

She went back over to Bart's page and composed a private message.

"Dear Bart, I heard through the grapevine that you are now engaged, after only three months of dating, to the girl with the misspelled name and the orange, alien skin obtained from Planet Tannicus."

At this point, Eva poured her herself another glass of wine. She was on a roll.

"I find it interesting that you have made a lifelong commitment in such a short time when I couldn't get you to make a decision about marriage in almost six years of dating! I see that she is a receptionist at the local gym.

Oh, the fascinating conversations you will have when she gets bored with you in the bedroom. And, I'm sure she will never, ever enjoy giving you head the way I faithfully did as a prelude to our passionate weekends.

- And, as you will remember, I do give a world class blow job. I just wanted to make you aware that you can kiss those things good-bye without first finding they will soon come with a much higher price tag. I never asked you for a thing. Not one damn thing, but I bet she does.

I'll just wager, in some small, dark part of your imagination, you are already worried, wondering how you are going to continue to keep this little tramp interested when your credit cards are all maxed out and you actually have to live on your sorry-ass second-rate accountant's salary. What will happen then?

I hung with you no matter how little money you made. I would have been with you for a lifetime because I loved you. I'm a stupid, pathetic little romantic that way. But, now I'm over it. Have a nice life in your soon-to-be sexless state and enjoy your ulcer. XOXO – Eva."

"That is fan-fucking-tastic! Poetry! I ought to write books!" She yelled and hit "send" with an evil cackle. She only wished she had a best girlfriend to high-five her and cheer her on. She fell back into her large couch cushions and laughed herself to tears. She knew he would "unfriend" her within the next few hours and block her within the next 24. More tears followed that thought.

Chester hopped up on the coffee table and rubbed against the laptop screen. He tasted the bits of chicken left from the almost empty plate. Sniffed disinterestedly at the wine glass and then leapt onto Eva's lap.

He stood up on his back legs and put his front paws on her shoulders and nuzzled her neck. He seemed to know when she was feeling down. He always made her feel better. She stroked his soft head and scratched his neck the way he liked.

He settled down next to her on the couch. She petted her cat and listened to the sound of canned laughter as some sitcom replayed on the television. After a while, she dried her tears and gathered up her dishes to take them to the kitchen.

Chester trailed behind her. He wound around her feet as she moved about the small area. She looked down at him before she turned off the kitchen lights.

"What's up with you, Chester? You're not usually this needy." Chester looked up at her and meowed.

They both came to a halt at the French doors. Now that night had fallen, she couldn't see farther than her motion sensor lights could reach. It suddenly occurred to her that her back patio was awash in bright light.

Something had set off her motion sensor lights.

Chester ran to the doors. Staring into the backyard, he began a strange sound in the back of his throat. It sounded sort of like a low, choked growl. It escalated to a series of loud cat growls. It was decidedly creepy and raised goose bumps on her skin.

She cautiously peered out into the night between the slats of her open blinds. The fog bank had drifted to just outside the reach of the patio lights. Within the swirl of fog, she thought she saw a figure, but she couldn't be certain. She blinked twice and the figure was gone. Only the fog bank remained. She moved her gaze from one side of her back yard to the other. There was nothing in either of her neighbors' back yards. The fog swirled almost like smoke, but there was no fire.

"Weird." She whispered. An involuntary shudder rattled her. She crossed her arms and hugged herself.

Chester suddenly settled down and stopped his yowling. He stared for a long time, but finally shrugged it off and moved back to his spot on the couch. She closed the blinds.

After she had enjoyed a long, hot bath, she crawled into bed. Her previous emotional rant had left her exhausted. Later, she would not remember falling asleep, but she would remember the dream.

She dreamt she was sitting in a private, theater balcony box. It was an old and ornate theater – huge, crystal chandeliers, heavy, tasseled curtains, and gilded moldings. It reminded her of the Orpheum in Memphis, Tennessee.

Her grandmother, who was far more open-minded than her mother, had taken her to see Rocky Horror when she was fifteen. Her mother had a fit when she realized later what they had gone to see.

In the dream, Eva was unaware of what was playing onstage. She was only aware that she was joined by a tall stranger. He stayed in the shadows. She could not see his face and could barely discern the outline of his shoulders in a black tuxedo. The crisp white shirt stood out in contrast.

Though she could not see his face, she could feel his eyes. His gaze moved over her and she could feel it like a physical touch everywhere he looked. His touch, light as down, moved across her lips and over her throat. She gasped as his gaze moved over her breasts and down her abdomen. She held her breath as it moved to her waist and finally to the place in her lap where her green satin dress pooled like an emerald oasis. Her face reddened with both arousal and embarrassment. She moaned aloud in both surprise and pleasure as she felt a monstrous orgasm building.

Fully clothed, and without any physical contact, the stranger brought her to a gasping, groaning orgasm.

When the last spasms of the orgasm stilled, she looked out over the edge of her balcony box. People in the seats below were staring up at her. Humiliation heated her face. She looked to the stranger, who now held the most perfect red rose she had ever seen. He stood and approached her. She wanted to look up at his face, but her eyes were riveted to the rose he carried.

He brushed the fragrant flower against each of her breasts in turn. She moaned softly as her breasts grew heavy and her nipples hardened like pebbles against the fabric of her dress. He laid the rose on her lap, with the stem pointing out toward her knees and the flower lying directly on top of her *mons veneris*.

Before letting go of the rose, he stroked the flower over the sensitive spot and she felt it as if she was naked. She whimpered. She wanted more and was ashamed that she should want something like this from a stranger in a public place. He bent down and whispered a single word which stayed with her and echoed into her waking moments.

Mine.

Eva awoke in the morning aroused and confused. At some point during the night, she shucked her shorts and tank top and was naked beneath her covers. She sat up in bed just as her alarm went off.

Eventually, she entered her kitchen and got the cat food down as Chester meowed relentlessly because she was not serving breakfast quickly enough to suit him. Showing no gratitude whatsoever, he immediately pounced on his food dish when she filled it. He ignored her. Eva ignored him back and made herself the routine maple and brown sugar oatmeal and her favorite Sumatra blend coffee.

After breakfast, she opened her blinds and went completely still as she looked out onto her back patio.

Her heart began to pound wildly against her ribcage.

She had a small café table with two matching chairs on her patio. Now, her eyes locked onto the table. Lying in the center like an understated centerpiece, was a single, perfect red rose.

Her trembling fingers unlocked one of the French doors. She opened it and stumbled outside, nearly losing her bathrobe in the process. She hastily tightened the sash as she approached the table. She lifted the bloom to her nose and inhaled its heady scent. She looked around her yard and did not find any evidence of her admirer.

She went back inside and locked the door behind her.

Even psychopaths know how to make romantic overtures.

She still found the gesture seductive. A shared memory of an evening's pleasure with an alluring stranger. She was an avid reader of fiction, so she found she accepted the bizarre nature of the situation in stride. She went to the kitchen and found pretty little crystal bud vase.

She ran the end of the rose's stem beneath a tepid tap and snipped the stem to a length suitable for the vase. *Thanks, Mama. This was one of the few nice things you ever taught me to do.* She put water in the vase and placed the flower in its new home. In a moment of romantic inspiration, she dashed to her bedroom and dug through her hair accessories, where she found a red satin ribbon to tie around the vase.

At work, Eva placed the rose on her desk. Stanley, who had been working on a spreadsheet, stopped when she came in. From his vantage point in the cubicle across from hers, he watched her carefully place her flower where she could look at it.

"Nice flower. Special occasion?"

She smiled and gently touched a petal. "No special occasion. I think I must have a secret admirer. He left it for me to find this morning."

"Really? Well, he needs to cut that shit out. He'll make the rest of us look bad," Stanley chuckled at his own joke. He was about to return to his work when he stopped to look more closely at her.

She thought again how subtly handsome he was. His dark blonde hair was an ordinary shade. His features came together in an expressive and intelligent, but average face. He was not a man that women would salivate over, but the longer one pondered him the more one realized how handsome he really was. His silver eyes now roamed over her face.

"Hey, did you do something different with your hair?"

She absently touched her long, brown hair. She usually kept it put up for work, but today she left it hanging around her shoulders.

"I left my hair down. That's all. Nothing special."

"It looks nice," he said. He hesitated as if he wanted about to say more, but he went back to his spreadsheet instead. Ever since he was promoted to be the supervising paralegal two years ago, he was more careful about what he said at work.

Too careful, Eva thought. She always knew there was something between them. They used to have coffee together before work. They used to be budding friends with the possibility of more. She sighed.

When she was certain Stanley was completely engaged with his work again, she nonchalantly pulled out a compact mirror from her purse. She gazed at her reflection and was surprised. Her brown hair seemed more lustrous than usual. Her blue eyes sparkled. She smiled and added a touch of lipstick. She did not look so "librarianesque" today. Librarianesque, was a term she overheard a couple of co-workers use to describe her in the ladies' room one day.

She had been sitting in a stall and had overheard Rachel Echols tell Heather Watanabe to "take her hair down." When Heather asked the reason, Rachel said, "You look like Eva Shelby with your hair up like that. Do you really want to look so librarianesque?"

Today, she felt unrestrained and passionate. She felt like one of the heroines of her favorite vampire novels. She felt desired. In the world of her small work cubicle, Eva turned on a little lamp she had brought from home when she began working at the law firm five years ago.

Normally, the job was hectic with work being interrupted by wave after wave of calls from anxious clients, medical providers, and insurance adjusters. She was one of the luckier paralegals. Her cubicle sported the one accessory which managed to stabilize her sanity – a window.

Her window overlooked the well-manicured grounds and fountain at the front of the building. While newbies and interns, if they were lucky enough to have a cubicle with a window, usually had an uninspiring view of the parking lot.

She ignored her calls. She spent her day catching up on filing and staring out the window at the grounds which were bursting with spring. Buds had just begun to appear on the trees and early annuals were flaring to life. The birds had returned and she could see them hopping around on the ground looking for bugs or seeds.

She watched co-workers take their breaks outside at the picnic table. The soul bright sunshine danced off their smiling faces. Winter had been too long this year. There was a need to be outdoors.

Her eyes moved from the window to the walls that surrounded her. Fabric covered cubicle walls. She had pinned up some pictures and a calendar with exotic pictures of beautiful, foreign lands she knew she would probably never see. *I can dream*, she thought, *no one can stop me from dreaming.*

At five o'clock, Eva felt as if she had been released from some tether to which she'd been fighting the reach all day. Stanley poked his head into her cubicle as she was preparing to leave. "He must really be some kind of guy."

"Who?"

He nodded toward her rose. "Your secret admirer. You've been all dreamy and zoned out today."

"Have I?" She hadn't realized Stanley was watching her.

"I'm the boss, right? I'm paid to notice shit like that."

She laughed. "Oh, it's just still new. I'm sure the shine will wear off once I see that he's just a regular guy who will cut and run when times get rough, or when something better comes along, the way that they all do."

Stanley scrunched his face up in an exaggerated wince and put his hand to his heart. "Ouch! Don't judge all of us by your ex. Generally, most consider me to be a good guy. Just ask my mom. My mommy thinks I'm very special." He said the last sentence with a babyish voice and a lisp – like a toddler.

Eva laughed aloud. "Noted. My apologies to you and your mommy."

He grinned and tapped a knuckle against the "doorway" to her cubicle. "Have a good weekend, Eva." There was another moment when he seemed to want to say something more – Eva found herself *wishing* he would say more – but then he turned away.

"You, too," she called to his retreating back.

Although the evenings were still a little chilly, as spring was still new, she decided to take her supper out onto the patio. She had made a lovely homemade vegetable soup and she enjoyed it with a BLT sandwich. She sipped a glass of *Pinot Grigio* and felt positively decadent.

The only drawback to the whole experience was the fact that Chester apparently felt abandoned and he stood at the door looking out at her, petulantly. "Sorry, Chester. This is Mommy's 'me' time," she said as she raised her wine glass to him in a salute.

From where she sat at the café table, she could gaze off into the backyard where she had seen the fog bank the night before. She thought again about the figure she had seen moving in the fog.

She was almost certain it had been a man. She recalled, from her extensive knowledge of vampire novels, the original Dracula story wove the legend that Dracula could call the fog to conceal him. He could also take on the appearance of a bat or a wolf. He could also call on those creatures to help him.

She wondered about this. It seemed most legends had some portion of truth seeded benignly within them. *This is silly. Vampires are not real. They are just dangerous and sexy stories. What brought on this line of thought?* She laughed at her own musing.

She scanned her back yard for signs of the fog bank. She was decidedly relieved to see no sign of it, but then a ripple of anxiety crawled up the back of her neck. She realized it was not dark yet.

She heard the phone ringing inside the house. She was surprised to notice she had forgotten her cell phone. She sighed, gathered up her dishes and went inside, nearly tripping over Chester as she made her way to the kitchen. She groaned when she saw the caller ID.

She lifted the phone to her ear to answer, "Hi, Mom."

"Eva Louise Shelby! Why do I have to stalk my own daughter to get her to talk to me? Your brother Johnathan calls me every other day."

Eva washed her dishes with the phone on her shoulder. "I talked to you yesterday, Mom."

"Yes, but I've called you twice. You never call me first anymore."

"Mom, why do I need to call when you I know you'll call *me* first? You never give me a chance to call you." Eva went about cleaning up her kitchen. The conversation was on autopilot. She'd been through it too many times before.

"Do you think you might be able to come see me this weekend?"

Eva winced at the hopeful note in her mother's voice. "Mom, Dad died almost 20 years ago. Don't you think you need to find some activities that don't involve me or Johnathan?"

"I don't know what you mean! I have my church group."

"That's nice, Mom, but don't you think you need to make some friends your own age to do things with? You know, like go movies or concerts. Things like that. You and Dad used to love going to movies."

"Don't you want to spend time with me?" Her mother's voice held the wavering note Eva dreaded.

"Of course, I want to spend time with you, Mom. It's just that I have a life of my own now. Plus, I live nearly 300 miles away. It's almost time to come home by the time I come see you. I usually wait for those nice, three day weekends where I can spend some real time with you." Eva patted herself on the back. *That was a nice save, if I do say so myself.*

It appeared to work, as her mother sniffed, but sounded more cheery. "Well, I guess I see your point. God knows your brother never comes home any more since he married that Chelsea two years ago." Eva's mother went on about the latest thing "that Chelsea" had done to offend her.

Eva only half listened as she realized full dark had fallen and her patio light was on.

Her heart sped up a couple a beats. Chester slowly backed away from the French doors and began a low growl. His fur fluffed up considerably.

"I have to go, Mom. "

She edged up to the French doors and peered outside. The light went out. She could not see anything with all the lights on in her kitchen and living room. She walked around and turned off her lights to let her eyes adjust.

She stood at the French doors. The fog bank had gathered in the middle of her back yard. Fear turned her knees to water. She barely had the strength to stand.

Last night, the fog had been at the far edge of her property line, near the woods which was about twenty yards from her back door. Now, the fog back was about halfway to her house.

It was edging closer.

The fog swirled and glimmered in the moonlight. Whatever material the fog was made of - it reflected light. Rolls and crests moved within the mass in a hypnotic – almost soothing – rhythm. She sensed raw and repressed power emanating from within. It somewhat reminded her of a gray ocean. The mass was also thick. She could not see anything of her yard past the fog bank except the tops of the trees, which towered behind the mass, at the edge of her property.

There was definitely a figure within. A tall man who stood very still.

She knew he could see her even though she had all her lights off and had backed away from the window. She trembled in fear as she felt his gaze. In a surge of strength, curiosity, and anger, she wanted to demand that he speak and identify himself.

She opened the back door and stepped out onto the patio, which set off her lights. She could still see the fog bank, but the figure had disappeared.

"Who are you?" She questioned the dark. "What do you want?"

The fog bank silently swirled and rolled. No answer was forthcoming.

That night, after snuggling down beneath her blankets, she had a similar dream as the one from the night before. The stranger was more solid and there was an orchestra playing on the stage. He timed her climaxes to the crescendos and her cries of passion were not so easily heard by the crowd below.

He laid the rose on her lap and whispered, "Mine."

When he moved to leave her, she tentatively reached out and caught his hand to delay him. He stopped, but did not turn around. She felt as if her heart would break if she let him leave.

"Please, stay with me or take me with you," she implored, softly. She was not sure if he heard her over the music.

There was a long pause. He gently tugged his hand free of her grip. "When it is time, I will take you with me. This is not the time."

"Why? Why can't I go now?" Tears rolled down her face and dropped onto her dress.

"You are not ready."

"Please!" She begged as he walked away.

Eva awoke to a gray dawn. She was grief stricken and aroused and she stifled a scream when she realized she was lying on her patio. Naked. Her discarded robe lay beside her and she was on her back with her legs spread. Across her belly - lay two perfect roses.

She sat up and grabbed her robe. She wiped her tears and looked around the yard. Her neighbors did not appear to be up yet and there was no fog. Fear took her in icy clutches as she slipped on her robe and slowly stood.

She was stiff and sore. She was terrified at the thought of how long she might have been lying outside. She was far more frightened of the fact that she had no idea how she got there. She had no memory of getting up and going to the patio.

She had no history of sleep walking. Luckily, her patio had a waist-high brick wall that lined the edge of her patio all around with one opening to the yard. She hoped she would not have been as visible as she feared.

The French doors were open. She went inside her house. Locked her doors, and closed her blinds.

It suddenly occurred to her that her cat was nowhere around. "Chester?"

Her heart took up a panicked beating as she searched her house. She finally found him under her bed. He was too frightened to come out. He hissed and backed up every time she tried to reach for him.

She decided to let him chill out while she took a shower. He finally crept into the kitchen around the time she was making breakfast. He seemed unusually nervous. He jumped at every noise.

She filled his food dish and was relieved when he let her pet him. She whispered soothing words to her furry baby and he leaned in to the comfort of her hand. *Looks like we're making each other feel better.*

She turned on the television, but could not focus. A terrible headache was taking root in her temples. She was tired, but afraid to go to sleep.

What would happen if I decided to do another erotic patio performance in the middle of the day when my neighbors are grilling their hamburgers? She wondered, with greasy, sick twinge in her stomach. She decided a shower might make her feel better. She enjoyed the hot spray of the shower and the cocooning steam that enveloped her.

Afterward, she cleaned off a spot on her fogged bathroom mirror and caught a glimpse of herself. *I might feel like shit,* she thought, *but I look fantastic! Better than I ever have.* Beneath the glow of the crystal globes above her bathroom mirror, she stared at her reflection in wonder.

Her blue eyes were luminous and her skin was clear and flawless.

As she dried her hair, she noticed the normal mousy shade of brown was now a glossy chestnut. When dried, her hair hung about her shoulders in loose waves. In the past, she could have never have achieved that effect if she had managed to attempt it by design.

She did not how it was possible, but she was certain her new appearance had something to do with the fog bank and the man in her dreams. She stared into her mirrored reflection and touched her face and hair with fingers that trembled in both fear and wonder. *What if I am losing my mind? What is happening to me?* Her stomach clenched at the thought.

After she was bathed and dressed, Eva was at a loss. Usually, she had a strict routine. On Saturdays, she went to the grocery store and she cleaned her house so that she could relax and enjoy her Saturday evening and Sunday.

Today, however, she did not feel particularly motivated. She ordered a medium pizza with all her favorite toppings for lunch – normally, completely forbidden because of the calorie count and being outside her tight budget – and she devoured it as if she had not eaten in weeks.

As she ate, she pulled out her laptop and she and Chester checked out Facebook. She noticed her ex had unfriended her. *No big surprise there.*

When she tried to send him a message, she discovered she was blocked. It should have devastated her. However, all she felt was a mere ache that gathered like a lump of her mother's dry Thanksgiving turkey in her throat. It did not take long before it loosened and dissipated.

Despite the ache, she was not sorry about the message she sent that caused Bart's harsh reaction. Her anger might have even taken him aback. Normally, she was such a meek soul. Her anger had served as her backbone and she was glad she had told him how she felt.

Sometimes it is important that you let a man know when he is an asshole and has chosen the wrong path. He needed to be enlightened. I did him a service. Eva giggled. *I should bill him for my services as an advisor.*

After shutting down her computer, Eva went about her usual routine.

Afterward, after 3 p.m., she poured herself a glass of wine, which she took out to the patio with tentative steps. She did not see any fog. All of the plants and furniture on her patio appeared to be where they were supposed to be. She sat and propped her feet up on the opposite chair and stared off into the woods at the edge of her property line.

In the cheerful spring afternoon sunlight, things did not seem so bad. She felt almost normal. Her headache had faded. She wondered about fog bank. What was it? Where did it go when she couldn't see it? How could she make it go away?

She thought about her new and improved appearance. Did she want to make it go away if it didn't mean her any harm? Some part of her – the primal part, the "tiny voice" – knew the fog bank was dangerous. That primal, subconscious part of her knew there would be a price to pay for her new appearance and her growing sense of confidence.

The thought that frightened her the most was when she considered the cost. What did it want?

Lost in her thoughts, she forgot she had carried her phone outside with her and she jumped when she heard the ringtone. She looked. It was her mother. For a moment, she considered letting it go to voicemail.

Why do I put myself through this? Resigned to do her duty, she picked up the phone.

"Hello? Eva? Have you decided if you are going to come home this weekend? Why haven't you called me?"

"Mom, we went through this last night. I said I wanted to wait until the holiday weekend so that I can stay longer. That five-hour drive wears me out when I know I have to just about turn right around and come back."

The argument continued from there. Eva distracted her mother by asking about her brother. Her mother took the bait and began a 10-minute tangent about Johnathan's wife, "that Chelsea." Finally, Eva made the excuse that she needed to go to the store and managed to get off the phone.

It was dark by the time Eva returned home from the grocery store. The dark made her move faster to unload her bags. Her vivid imagination – honed from years of horror fiction – imagined the thick, gray fog reaching silently from beneath her car to snake around her ankles. She looked down. She saw nothing but her driveway. She shuddered, shook off the horrible thoughts, and hurried to carry her bags inside.

Chester was hungry and complaining when she came into the house. He meowed his displeasure. She scowled at him as she moved around the kitchen to put the groceries away.

"You could have at least offered to carry in the bags."

"Meow."

"You could do more to help around here, you little furry freeloader."

"Meow ... meow."

"Fine. Here's your dinner." She filled his food dish and gave him some fresh water. He dived at the bowl. She laughed and rolled her eyes.

Still full from the pizza she ate earlier, Eva decided she only wanted a glass of wine.

Chester suddenly looked up from his food dish and began to growl and hiss. He crept cautiously out of the kitchen and toward the French doors.

Abandoning her wine on the counter, she followed him as far as the doorway to the kitchen. She was afraid to get much closer. She could see the French doors from the doorway. Her heart took up a trip hammer beat. Her whole body began to tremble at what she saw.

The patio light had been tripped. The fog bank surrounded the edge of her patio. The swirling gray mass was a massive, swirling gray wall. She could not see past it. It choked out the moonlight, like prison walls surrounding her back patio. A gray tendril of the fog drifted out from the rest of the mass, like a tentacle. It reached her patio table and chairs. It nudged the chair closest to it. It swung wide and knocked the chair over. She jumped at the racket the metal chair made as it hit her concrete patio.

At the far right corner of her patio, where the shadows were deepest, a tall male figure coalesced. He was a silhouette within the fog.

-She gasped and stepped back toward the kitchen and turned off her light. She stood in the dark and shook in fear - too scared to look outside.

How does one fight such a thing? Was it even real? What did it want? She tried to imagine calling the police and a harsh laugh burst from her. *They would lock me up.* She knew no one could help her.

Chester ran from the doors and into her bedroom where she knew he would hide under the bed. It was his happy place. He felt safest there.

She wanted to join Chester but was afraid to cross the open area between the kitchen and the living room. She would have to pass the doors.

Eventually, she worked up the nerve to peek cautiously around the corner. The fog was gone. The lights were off. A relieved sob escaped her and she wiped tears from her eyes as she immediately went to the doors, closed the blinds, and made sure the doors were locked securely.

She forsook the wine and choose hot tea instead. She decided to go into her bedroom and watch television in bed. With her bedroom door closed and locked.

She fell asleep with the television on.

The dream was similar to the ones before. The stranger sat in the shadows. The boldest thing about him was crisp white shirt, which conveyed a ghostly glow in the dark corner of the balcony box. A soft shuffling of garments indicated he had shifted in his seat as he regarded her. Something was different – more intense – in his gaze. His eyes glowed yellow in the shadows. She trembled at the sight. She was mesmerized, even though part of her wanted to run.

The orchestra on stage played an intense piece, dramatic and difficult. She thought she recognized the fourth movement of Dvorak's *New World Symphony*. It was hard to decide on the exact movement because the crowd below was noisy as if the concert had not already started. The resulting din disoriented her.

Her attention was distracted from the concert as she was caressed by the stranger's gaze. Her breath caught. He rose from his seat and approached her. He was holding a perfect red rose.

He ran the blossom along her body and she moaned. He dropped the rose on the floor, gripped her hands, and pulled her to her feet. He turned her away from him, toward the railing of the balcony. With his hands on her waist, he guided her to the railing where she looked over the edge and down at the audience below.

The crowd quieted and looked up at her expectantly. She saw a sea of faces of all ethnicities. The faces were widely varied in appearance, but all seemed extraordinary in some fashion.

She gasped as the stranger suddenly pushed her forward at the waist and she was bent over the rail. He pushed her dress up and slid her panties down. She could feel cool air drifting over her naked buttocks and her exposed nether region.

Slowly, she felt herself being filled as he entered her from behind. He began to stroke slowly at first. The audience below watched as she found herself caught up in a whirling ecstasy. He began to thrust harder and faster.

She gripped the balcony rail for fear of being pushed over the top. She screamed her climax as the audience below watched and seconds later she felt his telltale shudder within her. When he was finished, he pulled her up straight and ripped her dress from her.

She cried out and tried in vain to cover herself with her hands. Her face flamed with the heat of humiliation. She was naked and exposed before the crowd. He whispered, "Mine," into the delicate cup of her ear just before he lifted her and threw her from the balcony.

She screamed as she fell but it was cut short as she was caught by hundreds of waiting, hungry hands. She was lowered, almost reverently, to the carpeted aisle. Then, the crowd descended upon her and she found herself being caressed and kissed.

Her arms and legs were spread open wide and every inch of her explored most intimately. She was made to climax again and again until she was nearly mad. The individuals in the crowd were whispering a single word repeatedly, "Mine."

She heard the word over and over in overlapping waves of whispers: *Mine, mine, mine, mine, mine, mine* ....

In the middle of one screaming orgasm, she awoke.

She was in the living room, splayed naked on the couch. She noticed bruises all over her. She was shaky and sore. She drew up in a ball and wept.

I'm losing my mind.

It was a long time before her tears dried up and she regained enough strength in her limbs so sit up. She stumbled to her bedroom and into the adjoining bathroom.

She turned on the bathroom light and examined herself in the mirror.

She looked even more beautiful than she had yesterday. She seemed to glow. The only flaws marking her were a series of small bruises all over her body. She found them everywhere – on her breasts, her thighs, her upper arms, her back and even her buttocks. As she strained to look at her backside in the mirror, she realized her hair had grown.

It was down below her shoulder blades and she was sure it was just at her shoulders a couple of days ago. She was tempted to cry again. Instead, she got into the shower and let the hot water wash away her worries.

After she dressed, she opened her curtains and blinds. The house was dark. She was shocked to find the sun had begun its journey toward the West.

Alarmed, she picked up her cell phone to look at the time. It was four o'clock on Sunday afternoon! She had slept for almost 20 hours! This had never happened to her before.

Suddenly, she realized she had not seen Chester. *Oh, my poor baby must be so hungry*! She called him. At first, there was no answer. She eventually heard a small mewling, like a frightened kitten. She followed the sound to find Chester in a far corner under her bed.

At age of seven, Chester was long past the kitten stage, but he was mewling and refused to be touched. Eva did not want to force him. She went to the kitchen and filled his food dish. She was considering something to prepare for herself when she heard a knock on her front door.

She opened the door to find Stanley outside. Her appearance seemed to startle and mesmerize him. His mouth dropped open and it took him a moment to speak. She waited expectantly. Finally, he raised the book he had been holding.

"My girlfriend finished the book and I was returning it. I knew it was important to you."

She smiled at him. His thoughtfulness was sweet. "Thanks, Stanley, but you could have just brought it to work. You didn't have to make a special trip."

He shrugged. "I just knew your books were important to you so I thought I would bring it."

She accepted the book. "Thank you."

He started to turn away and leave, but stopped and turned back. "Eva, are you okay?"

Bemused, she tilted her head as she considered his question. "I think so. Don't I look okay?"

He laughed. She smiled when he even blushed. "Yes, you look okay. You look better than okay. You actually look great, but you seem different -- I'm not sure what it is, but you're just *different*."

"I'm fine. It must be the new boyfriend. He's having quite an effect on me."

"Maybe that's it," Stanley said. "He's a lucky guy."

"Thank you for saying so, " she trailed off, unsure of what to say next. Things had suddenly grown awkward.

"Well, I guess I had better get going. I'll see you at work in the morning." He waved as he walked away.

She waved back. "Bye, Stanley."

The sight of Stanley walking away had a peculiar effect on her. Her heart gave a little tug. Suddenly, on an impulse she did not entirely understand, she called out to him. He turned back, his expression both surprised and curious.

"Would you like to come in for just a minute? You can have a glass of wine and take a look at my book collection. There might be another book your girlfriend would like."

Stanley was still for a moment. She was sure he considered declining her invitation, but he walked toward her instead. She smiled and ushered him into the house.

She closed the door and laid her book on the bench by the door. Normally, she would have put it straight back among its companions on her bookshelf, but that didn't seem so important now.

Stanley acted slightly uncomfortable and unsure of himself. She also detected the slightest bit of guilt in the way he smiled and avoided her eyes.

It was the guilt that told her all she needed to know.

He was attracted to her. She smiled and forced herself to stop it from becoming a grin. The "thing" that was always between them was no longer a mystery to her. She indicated her bookshelves with a sweep of her arm.

"Go ahead and browse while I go get our wine."

He dutifully began studying the books on the shelves as she went to the kitchen. She watched him through the open kitchen door as she poured two glasses of wine. He was tallish – standing about six feet tall.

Although it was spring, he still wore tan corduroy trousers. Normally, he wore a neutral, broadcloth shirt, tie, and a sweater vest that matched his trousers. However, that was on a workday. Today was not a workday so he wore simple, dark green shirt, untucked.

She brought him his glass of wine. As he turned to take it, Eva again took note of the one truly extraordinary feature Stanley possessed. His eyes.

His silvery-gray eyes were framed in thick, dark lashes. He was normally a kind and mild-mannered man. However, he did not get to be the supervising paralegal by being meek.

He could be surprisingly aggressive and intimidating when the situation warranted. Eva performed her job with extreme efficiency, but she did make a mistake now and again. Even she had found herself impaled on his silver laser gaze on occasion.

His unexpected ability to be authoritative was something that had both amazed and mystified her. Luckily, most of the time, he was just easy-going, kind-hearted Stanley.

As he accepted the wine glass from her, Eva realized she saw something new upon which to speculate. Desire. He cleared his throat and looked back toward the sea of titles. "I don't even know where to begin to pick another book for her."

Eva moved over to the sofa and sat down. "Tell me a little bit about what she speaks of when she talks about the Twilight books. Maybe, I can pick up something from that which will tell me what she might like to read next."

Stanley appeared to think about this as he moved to sit beside her, while keeping a respectable distance, on the couch. "She mostly talked about the characters, but she especially went on about the relationship between the two main characters."

"She likes the romance of the story, eh? If that's true, then she would probably enjoy the Sookie Stackhouse vampire novels by Charlaine Harris," Eva said. She placed her wine glass on the coffee table and got up to get the first couple of books. She put them on the coffee table in front of Stanley.

"Thanks, Eva. You picked those just from what I told you?" He appeared to be impressed with her quick assessment.

She sat back down on the couch, at a less respectable distance, next to him. "What you told me about her particular interest is what helped me decide. If you had said she was particularly interested in the vampires then I probably would have picked something else, like Anne Rice's stuff. You said she was interested in the romance. There is something very sexy about having someone strong and mysterious find you to be special."

"Suddenly, that makes me feel insecure." He laughed, but she could see that a nerve had been tweaked.

"Don't feel insecure. It's a fantasy. Don't you have a fantasy? Harmless stuff."

"My fantasies don't involve strong vampire guys."

It was Eva's turn to laugh. "Then what do you fantasize about?"

She laughed in amazement as he blushed. She could not resist teasing him, "*This* very situation is a fantasy of yours, isn't it? I can tell by the way you're blushing!"

"Bullshit! I am not blushing." He said as he flushed a deeper shade of red. He took a long sip of his wine. He had nearly finished his glass by the time his blush faded.

"With those eyes of yours, I could see you being the object of a fantasy or two ..." she said. She let the sentence trail off.

She could not understand how or why she was being so bold. She just found herself inexplicably drawn to Stanley. She had always been drawn to him, but tonight was different. She wanted -- she refused to think about what she wanted.

The moment had grown too intense. To ease his awkwardness, he reached for his wine glass and seemed surprised to find it empty.

She reached to take it and her hand brushed his. She leaned across him, her breast pressed against his arm. "Let me go get you a refill."

She rose with both glasses. He rose and followed her to the kitchen. "You don't have to do that. I'm driving and I should probably get going."

She placed the wine glasses down on the counter. She could not hide her disappointment. She felt strangely reckless. "Do you really have to leave or am I making you uncomfortable?"

Startled by her candor, he looked directly into her eyes and she saw hunger and desire there. She also saw a man struggling with indecision. "Both."

"Why do I make you uncomfortable?" She stepped closer. He didn't back away.

His eyes had not left hers. "I think you know why."

She waited. She did not want to push. She wanted him to be brave enough to do what she knew he wanted to do – to do what *she* wanted him to do. He slowly reached out and took a strand of her hair and rubbed it between his fingers.

She held her breath as his eyes roamed her face. His hand followed as he gently stroked her cheek and cupped her chin. She reached for him, placing her hands on his waist.

She watched an intensity grow in his eyes and he closed the distance and lowered his mouth to hers. The kiss was tentative at first as he tested her mouth to seek a good fit. The kiss deepened when she responded with a groan and opened her mouth.

She thought her knees would buckle as he pulled her in close and entangled his hand in her hair. What came next shocked her. She had never in her life behaved with such wild abandon and she found that Stanley surprised her with an animal-like voraciousness – something she would never have expected from him.

Once it began, he never hesitated again.

"Where's your bedroom?" He growled against her neck.

She took his hand and led the way. Once inside the room, he closed the door behind him and pulled her to him. He kissed her as he pulled her blouse over her head and tossed it to the floor. She was glad she had chosen to wear a pretty bra that day.

He ran his hands over the smooth, satin cups, then he let his fingers trail over the smooth satin of her skin as he touched the tops of her breasts. Her breath caught as he touched her. She looked up into his eyes.

His mesmerizing silver eyes crinkled at the corners as his face transformed with a wicked grin. "Don't forget to breathe, Eva."

She let out a shaky breath she did not even realize she had been holding.

He slid the straps of her bra down, then hooked his fingers into the edges of the bra and tugged downward until her bare breasts spilled out over the top of the cups. His gaze drank in the sight. His hands stroked her skin and trailed teasing touches across her nipples.

She reached around behind her to unhook and remove her bra, but he stopped her. "Not yet, Eva. Leave it just like that for now."

She obeyed and reached to unbutton his shirt instead. His opened shirt revealed a lightly furred and surprisingly well-muscled chest. She slid his shirt backward down off his shoulders and helped him unbutton the cuffs.

He tossed the shirt to the floor. He walked her backward toward the bed and unbuttoned the top of her jeans as he went. He slid the zipper down, grasped the waist and tugged her pants down to mid-thigh. He grabbed the edges of her panties and did the same.

He pushed her backward until she fell onto the bed. He stood over her. His silver eyes practically glowed with intensity. He studied every inch of her that was revealed. She could almost feel his hungry gaze.

It reminded Eva of her dream.

Stanley pulled out his cell phone. "I find this incredibly sexy ... all your private parts are revealed to me, but you're still half dressed. It seems more indecent than actually being naked. I want to take a picture of you. Will you let me?"

Completely aroused, she nodded, but covered her face with her hands. She heard the telltale shutter sounds as he took three pictures of her at various angles. He laid the phone on her nightstand.

She uncovered her face as she felt him pull her jeans and panties off with one final tug. She gasped as he turned her over onto her stomach. He unfastened her bra and ran his hands down the length of her body, kneading her buttocks and thighs.

She could not stifle her groan of pleasure as he pushed her legs apart. He slowly, and thoroughly, explored her first with his fingers. She felt his questing fingers part her nether lips and then enter her. He pushed two fingers within her in several long, strokes until she was thoroughly ready. She cried out for more.

She could not quite believe this was actually happening. He turned her onto her back. She watched him slowly remove his trousers and boxers to reveal his erection. This time it was her hungry gaze that drank in the sight of him.

There was no hesitation as he pushed her thighs apart and moved between them. He lowered his mouth to her nipples, giving each one his undivided attention until she thought she would lose her mind. Finally, he kissed her and then raised up to look into her eyes as he pushed all the way into her.

She cried out in pleasure and arched against him. She was restlessly moving beneath him. She wanted release from the pressure she could feel building.

"Shhh. Take it easy, Eva. Let *me* do the work. I want it too, baby. Just hang onto me. We'll get there. I promise," Stanley murmured into her feverish mouth as he kissed her again, deeply.

She did as he instructed and hung on to his hips. He pushed her legs up and placed them on his shoulders, which brought her hips up and allowed him access to push into her as deeply as he could. When he began to move, he rocked both of their bodies to a unique and perfectly synchronized rhythm.

The climax was explosive. She came first and her convulsive shudders of pleasure brought him over the edge and he cried out and clutched her tighter as he pumped his release into her. She held onto him until both their shudders subsided.

Afterward, they enjoyed each other in the form of drowsy touches. They did not speak for the longest time. She had no words for what had happened, and she suspected Stanley didn't either. She knew quite suddenly that she could easily love him if she didn't already.

Who are you kidding, Eva? Stop lying to yourself. You've been in love with this man for a long time.

For five years, Stanley had been her friend and her co-worker. He had been her boss for the past two years. He was a good man. He was familiar, but he was not hers. Not yet, anyway. She felt guilty.

She had met his girlfriend, Shannon, and even liked her. *Still, a girlfriend isn't a wife, right?* Eva told herself. It didn't help.

They were lying on their sides, facing each other. She could see the clock on her nightstand over Stanley's bare shoulder. It would be dark in less than an hour. She thought of her other lover. She knew he would be coming for her soon. She shivered.

She briefly wondered if she could convince Stanley to stay the night. She thought of the fog and the stranger and she almost ready to beg Stanley to stay with her. Each night it had edged closer. What would be next? Could it get into her house? Some instinct told her that it could not come in unless she invited it. However, she was frightened to think she may not be able to resist its pull.

"Are you okay?" Stanley asked.

She touched his face as she studied it. The fiery light from the setting sun came through her bedroom window and created an interesting play of light and shadow across his expression as it was filtered through the blinds. She touched his cheek.

"I'm fine."

He looked at her arm, which he was in the process of stroking. "I noticed you have several small bruises all over you. Where did you get those? Have you taken up kickboxing or something?"

She strongly considered tossing a joke back to him about kickboxing or a massage gone terribly wrong, but instead she decided to tell him the truth. "I honestly don't know where they came from. I've been having some odd dreams lately and walking in my sleep. It's getting to be a little scary, actually. Anyway, I woke up with those today and I have no idea what I did to get them. Maybe I fell or something."

"*What?*" Alarmed, Stanley raised up on his elbow. "Eva, you need to see a doctor about this. You could get seriously hurt!"

"I know. It's okay. It just started last Thursday. I'm going to call my doctor next week. It will be okay."

"You promise?"

She smiled. It was nice to have someone (other than her mother) to be concerned about her. "I promise."

He looked relieved.

She changed the subject. "What about you? Are you okay?"

Before he could answer her question, his cell phone beeped. He turned over and picked it up from where he left it on her night stand. She caught a glimpse of the erotic picture of he had taken of her. She blushed.

Stanley had gotten a text message. She could see the guilt on his face.

"It's Shannon. She's wondering where I am. I was supposed to meet her at her place a half hour ago. We were going to go out to dinner."

Eva sat up. "Then you need to get going."

He rose from the bed and gathered his clothes. She enjoyed the view. He tilted his head in the direction of her bedroom door. "Do you mind if I use your bathroom?"

"That's fine." She rose from the bed, still naked, and showed him where to find things in the bathroom. She heard the shower running as she straightened her room and put her clothes back on.

He emerged ten minutes later. She handed him the novels she wanted to loan Shannon. He took them awkwardly.

The sun had set and a twilight blue/gray light held full darkness at bay for the moment. They stood on her front porch, unsure of what to do. Finally, he reached out and they embraced for a long moment.

He started to say something, but she interrupted, "Don't say anything right now, Stanley. Let time figure this one out. I think there is something strong and real between us, but I know there are other factors in place right now. Let's allow time to let those factors play themselves out. Until then ... we will just accept what we have with great -- affection."

Stanley paused as he thought about it. "I think I can live with that for now."

She waved good-bye when he turned to look at her just before he climbed into his car. He waved and afforded her a small smile. After he left, she went inside, shut the door and leaned against it. She wanted to cry. She wanted to call him and ask him to come back. She wanted to tell him she was scared about what might happen if she was left alone in the fog. She hoped that somehow everything would work out.

"*Meow.*"

Deep in thought, she was startled by her cat. She looked toward the living room to see that Chester had ventured out. He was cautiously slinking toward the kitchen where his food dish awaited. She followed him and spoke soothingly as she made herself a glorious salad, which she enjoyed out on the patio after righting the chair knocked over the previous night. She had worked up an appetite and found she was famished.

She refused to be frightened off her own patio.

Even when she was jolted by the site of a dozen gorgeous red roses on the patio table. She moved the roses out of the way to make room for her salad dish and her wine glass.

In regards to her lover who hid within the fog, she did not know what was happening to her or if it was even real, but she knew those flowers were real. Hence, she had to believe that her lover was real. She wondered when he felt she would be ready. What was the criteria?

She thought about her life and all the things she would never do just because life was not what she expected it to be. She thought about her calendar at work. This month, the picture was a beautiful mountain view from the Isle of Skye. She wiped tears as she thought about how she knew that, barring some miracle, she would never visit it.

She was in debt with school loans, a car, a mortgage, and simple living expenses. She was a slave to her debts with no end in sight as to when she might manage to dig her way out.

She thought again about Stanley. She still felt a lingering tingle from their encounter. She refused to shower just yet and wash away the evidence of his touch. She wanted to keep his scent on her and the evidence of his passion inside her for a while longer.

She knew that in all likelihood, he would rationalize himself back to remaining with his girlfriend rather than making a big, difficult decision. That's what men always did, at least in her past experience. She just didn't see any hope of being with him.

Her cell phone began going off inside the house.

She could not believe she had forgotten it again. She considered rushing to it, but really didn't want to. Instead, she enjoyed her wine and her salad. Finally, as dark approached, she took her empty dishes into the kitchen, washed them and put them away. She made another trip outside to gather her roses. She put them in the prettiest crystal vase she owned.

She turned on her television for the background noise.

After he had finished his meal, Chester allowed her to pet and comfort him. She kissed him and stroked his soft fur before depositing him into her room. She encouraged him to scoot under the bed.

Eva took off all her clothes, and slipped on a lovely red, silk robe that she had only saved for weekend trips when she and Bart were still together. It was long past nightfall when she wandered into the living room and checked her phone.

Her mother had called. Twice. She put the phone back down. It was time for her mother to learn to live her own life.

Charles Kellerman was ending his news broadcast on the television, "From our family to yours, good evening." She turned off the television with the remote.

"Good night, Charles," she whispered.

Although she expected it, she still gasped a little when the patio lights clicked on. The fog bank was right outside the doors. The swirling gray mass pressed against the glass of her French doors. The larger, male figure was in the center of the mass. She did not realize she had made a choice until it was made.

She was tired of fighting. She was tired of being afraid.

It was on trembling legs that she walked to the doors and opened them. She took a few steps back as the fog swirled into the house. The fog surrounded her. It pressed against her. It was then she realized it was not fog.

This was - something else.

The stranger stood before her. She still could not see his face. His features were indistinct. He brought his hand up to cup her chin. He bent forward to kiss her lips. He was merely a shadow.

She had read about vampires for so many years. She thought she knew what to expect, but now she suddenly had doubts. She felt the first icy prickles of real terror. Mortal fear – she now understood the meaning of that phrase. Her stomach turned rancid and she felt her bowels heated up and threatened to loosen. Her muscles wanted to give out. She stood before the mysterious stranger and trembled like a terrified Chihuahua.

He tugged at the sash on her robe and it fell open. He pushed it from her shoulders and it fell into a crimson heap at her feet. He ran his fingers over her body. She gasped as he took her in his arms and lowered her to the floor. He pressed her knees apart. Her breath quickened. He suddenly dissolved and disappeared.

The fog itself began to press against her.

Suddenly, she knew.

All mythology had some root of truth that is distorted in the retelling. Such an ancient legend as the vampire myth had surely been misconstrued over time to become something unrecognizable from the truth. The mass swirling and whispering to her now was the truth. At first, its caress was gentle.

She was touched all over. Covered by the fog. It was more like a giant, moist second skin as it adhered itself to her body.

Then, there was a bite. She yelped in pain.

Then, there was another bite and another and she was pushed down onto her back. She thrashed and fought. She tried to scream but the fog filled her mouth and throat.

The biting became internal. It was like hot lava poured through her, filling her mouth and throat.

The Fog took her over, entered her in every possible way. The pain was indescribable. The massive fog bank engulfed her. It attempted to crowd its mass into her human form. It poured into her through every orifice. Each orifice expanded and split far beyond human limits and then her skin dissolved beneath the hungry fog. It was a bath in boiling oil.

She struggled to breath and clawed at her face but the fiery bites were dissolving her hands. She felt her own wet, naked phalanges tearing at the dissolving skin of her face.

She could only create, inhuman choked sounds in her agony until the Fog managed to reach her brain and cut the ties to relieve her suffering.

Soon, she could not see because she no longer had eyes to do so. She felt no pain, but she was faintly aware of her body thrashing as it was taken apart like a cooked chicken. Finally, she gave in to the great blackness with a sense of relief.

She was not sure what time it was when suddenly she opened new eyes, but it seemed like a long time had passed.

She still retained her own consciousness. Her memory was intact -- but now she was also -- *Them*.

She was Joined.

She looked around and could see her living room from several viewpoints at once. The crystal vase, which held her roses, sparkled in the reflected moonlight from the open French doors.

She saw her robe on the floor. There was something unspeakably beautiful in the way the robe looked almost like shimmering liquid where it lay. Silk was such a luxurious fabric. She had not truly appreciated it before that moment.

She saw the spot where she had died such a short time ago. There was nothing left of her physical body, except for some waste and other sticky fluids, the sight of which disturbed her. She quickly looked away.

She flexed and stretched in her new form.

She felt powerful and dangerous. *You are dangerous, my darling*, They lovingly whispered to her. Life was vastly different and new.

We will walk our path together in this grand union. We will find others – other willing beings – who will strengthen our family.

First, her indulgent lovers wanted to take her someplace special. They knew everything about her, including her dearest heart's desires.

Let's go on a trip. We think it is time you got to see the world – and the world tour begins with the Isle of Skye. After that ... thanks to your earlier encounter, we already have considered a new lover to court.

Stanley is quite intriguing ... and we found that tiny sample he left to be quite tasty. We want more.

FOG BANK
PART II
The Seduction of Stanley

FOG BANK II:

THE SEDUCTION OF STANLEY

Stanley Crump rolled down his window as he drove home. It was as if he thought the wind could cast a net around his lust and guilt and sweep it all out of his car and into the night.

He felt guilty. Guilty. Guilty. Guilty. *What the hell had just happened?* His head was still reeling and his limbs retained the warm, languorous weakness that followed vigorous sex.

As he stopped for a red light, he looked at his hands on the steering wheel. His fingertips tingled as he remembered the feel of Eva's body beneath them. He had just stopped off at Eva's house to drop off the book he had borrowed on behalf of his girlfriend Shannon.

He ended up in Eva's bed.

They'd been co-workers and friends for several years. He had not realized how drawn he was to her until that evening. Something about her had changed in the last few days -- some swift and unmistakable transformation had taken place.

What began as an innocent visit ended as a huge transgression. *This isn't me.* His anguished thoughts threw him into an emotional spin. He was normally loyal. He had never cheated on a girlfriend before.

His cell phone interrupted his riotous thoughts. He picked it up out of the cup holder in the center console. The caller was Shannon, however, behind the caller's name was a background picture that nearly sent him into the nearest ditch if he had not regained control of the car.

The erotic picture he had taken of Eva just an hour or so before was his background wallpaper on the phone.

"Shit! How did that get put up as wallpaper?"

He fumbled with the phone as if it were a flapping fish and dropped it into the passenger floorboard. He missed Shannon's call. He pulled over at the nearest gas station. He unbuckled his seatbelt and leaned over to retrieve the phone.

He picked it up and checked. He saw the missed call from Shannon. She left a voicemail. He knew what that was about. She was worried. He was late picking her up for dinner.

He was puzzled to find the wallpaper on his phone was still set to the picture of him and Shannon taken at the riverside boardwalk last summer. It was their first date. To ease the awkwardness, he jokingly suggested they make a selfie to commemorate what could potentially be the best or the worst date of their lives. It turned out to be the best. She had him when she laughed and threw up a peace sign for the picture. He still smiled when he studied the picture ten months later.

He looked through his photo files and located the pictures of Eva. He had taken three pictures at various angles. He opened it and there she was. She was on the edge of her bed, lying back. Her feet were still dangling above the carpet and she covered her face with her hands.

Eva was still partially dressed, but all her private parts were erotically exposed. Her breasts spilled out over her bra, the straps and cups of which had been pulled down by his own hands just moments before the picture. Her jeans and panties were pulled down almost to her knees. Her dark pubic hair drew his eyes down to the spot above where her thighs met. The hair was not thick; he could easily make out the feminine folds beneath. Her thighs were parted just enough to see – He tore his eyes away from the photo as he realized he had grown hard again.

What am I doing? When did I become an asshole?

He immediately deleted all three photos – the second was a close-up view of one of her delectable nipples and the other was right above her thighs. He was dismayed and disgusted at his reluctance to delete the pictures. He felt marginally better after he deleted them, then he called Shannon.

Shannon didn't even say hello. "Please tell me you are wrapped around a tree because I will accept nothing less than your death, or at least some sort of dismemberment, as an excuse for being almost an hour late."

She sounded worried but was still playful. It was one of the many things he loved about her. *God, she's awesome*. The thought brought about a sickening sense of guilt.

Stanley chuckled. "I'm so sorry, baby. I stopped at Eva's house and she helped me pick out some more reading material for you. We got to talking and I was there longer than I expected. I am only about ten minutes away now."

"Well, as long as you come bearing good books, then I might be persuaded to forgive you *this* time," she managed to sound imperious, but he heard the warmth in her tone.

"Thank you, your highness. I shall approach upon my noble steed shortly," he managed a British accent – not an easy thing for a Southern man.

"Humph ..." she said and hung up.

He grinned and dropped his phone back into the cup holder. *Maybe I can get past this. I will forget what happened and never allow myself to get into that situation again.*

As soon as he arrived at Shannon's apartment complex, he knew he was being naïve. She waited on her balcony. He got out of his car when a sound made him glance up. She grinned and waved.

"Wait there! I'm starving! Keep the engine running! I'm coming down," she shouted, then disappeared into her apartment. She trotted down the stairs at an impressive rate of speed for a tall woman in high heels.

He got back into the car and started the engine. When she made it to the bottom of the stairs, she straightened her skirt and turned a full circle for his enjoyment. He could not suppress a smile at her antics, which of course, bumped up the level on his guilt-o-meter to ten.

Her honey-colored hair hung about her shoulders in soft waves. Her legs went on for miles in a yellow skirt that ended about mid-thigh. She wore a simple button up white floral blouse with a sexy lace camisole beneath. She wore a simple pearl necklace and matching bracelet. Her high heeled pumps matched the yellow skirt. Her dark eyes were full of playful mischief as she sauntered to the car. He got out, went around and opened the door.

In her heels, their eyes met at the same level. He placed a hand on her waist and a soft kiss on her mouth. He inhaled her perfume and tasted her sweet sigh and felt like a monster for the way he had betrayed her. Shannon Beckman was special. They had a great thing going and he screwed it up. She just didn't know it yet. He would never be able to sort out or explain what had happened with Eva.

She slid into the passenger seat and he rounded the front of the car and took his place behind the wheel. He had promised her Thai food at their favorite restaurant.

*****

Shannon made hungry growling sounds as she studied the menu at the Thai place. Stanley laughed and found she merely vocalized how he felt, too.

Yeah, great sex always makes me hungry. He thought, and then felt bad that his guilt did not kill his appetite.

They began with their favorites as appetizers – Chicken Satay and Thai spring rolls. After they had wiped out the appetizers, Shannon was still drooling and was as ready for her Pad Thai and he was for his Tom Kha Gai and Nam Tok Beef. Despite the fact that it was late for the dinner hour, the restaurant was still busy and lively with lots of background conversation, clinking plates, and music. The food, atmosphere, and the large front windows that provided them a nice view of the well-lit street and sidewalk, were all part of the package that made this restaurant one of their favorites.

Shannon gushed about the books Eva had sent for her to read. The moment was so normal Stanley could almost pretend nothing had changed. He and Eva were still just good friends and co-workers and Eva loaned Shannon fun books to read. Shannon was on a vampire kick and had just completed the Twilight series of books by Stephenie Meyer and Eva had loaned her the first couple of Sookie Stackhouse novels by Charlaine Harris. This was the reason he'd gone to Eva's house. He had borrowed the last Twilight book and had shown up to return it. Eva invited him in to make suggestions for new ones Shannon might like.

He was still not sure how he ended up in bed with Eva after such an innocent beginning. It was just that ... there was something new ... something irresistibly sensual about her lately and it drove him nuts. *What had changed?* He tried to put his finger on it.

He shook off his musings to tune back into Shannon as she had moved from books to her work. He would have to save his analysis of what had happened with Eva for later.

Abruptly, Shannon switched to her favorite subject – when she would begin college. She gave him sudden smile.

"Guess what I did today?"

"What?"

"I checked my savings account and ..." she left the sentence to dangle between them like a piece of yarn wiggled in front of a cat.

Stanley could feel his own expression erupt into a grin. "You finally have enough?"

"Yes! After five long years, I will finally have enough money to go to college," Shannon whispered, as if the words were part of a sacred spell that would be undone if not spoken reverently.

Unshed tears glimmered in her dark eyes that danced above the little flickering candle on the table between them.

He knew what this meant for her. She had slaved as a legal secretary to some of the most aggressive attorneys in town. She bought her clothes at thrift stores and she only ate out when Stanley paid for it. Otherwise, she cooked special meals for him using funds from her carefully dispersed budget. She was not so much frugal by nature as by design. She simply had to be. Her family lived in a small rural town outside of Nashville and she had no one to pay for her dream of becoming an attorney except for herself.

Stanley understood this dream. He had paid for his own education when he became a paralegal. He had considered taking his education further and going on to law school, but he made a good living at Hill, Druthers, and Matheson – the upscale law firm where he worked as the supervising paralegal. Now in his early thirties, he was content to continue his position at the firm. His salary was generous. However, he knew if the situation changed, he might consider going back to school.

He reached across the table to take Shannon's hand. "Congratulations! We will need to plan a little micro-trip – my treat, of course – to celebrate. Where would you like to go?"

Shannon's happy laugh was a sound of such sheer joy, he would have done anything to make her laugh that way again. She appeared to deeply consider his trip proposal. She started to laugh and covered her mouth – it was a self-conscious habit. He was certain she was unaware of it. He would bet she had worn braces as a child and the habit developed to cover any action that would expose her teeth more fully.

"What's so funny?"

She shook her head, but her eyes twinkled. "You'll think I'm too much of a dork."

"No more than I already do," Stanley said, smiling.

She laughed. "Okay ... I just suddenly thought of being on one of those old commercials – 'Shannon Beckman, you've finally saved enough for college. What do you want to do now?'"

"You want to go to Disney World," Stanley finished the commercial scenario for her.

At this point, she practically laid over the table laughing and giggling. "Yes. Yes, I do!"

He shook his head slowly, but could not stop grinning. "You're right, I think you just went up on my dork-o-meter, but if my lady wants to go to Disney World, then that is where I will take her."

"Yay!" She clapped.

He was surprised by his own laughter. It sounded carefree. Shannon's spark was contagious.

Unfortunately, a phone call on his cell ruined the moment for him.

It was a call from Eva and the background photo was the extreme close-up he had taken from right above the top of her thighs -- close enough to count the pubic hairs.

Luckily, he had put the phone on vibrate as he usually did during meals. He also had kept it in his pocket rather than put it on the table. When the phone went off, he felt the enthusiastic vibrations and subtly checked his phone. The picture gave him a jolt. *What the hell? I know I deleted those pictures!* He thought.

He silenced the call and let it go to voicemail, but the whole thing left him distracted and unsettled.

Shannon picked up on the change in him immediately. Her smile faded and her expression grew concerned. "Are you okay, honey? You got pale all of a sudden."

He forced a smile he was sure looked as stiff as it felt. "It's just work. The boss is putting pressure on me to run the end of the month stuff first thing tomorrow, but I am off work right now and I don't appreciate the interruption."

"They do that all the time. I know how much you hate that," Shannon's sympathy was genuine.

He felt like more of an asshole than ever. First, infidelity, now lies to cover the infidelity fallout. He hated to think of what he might be capable of next.

It was not long after that he chose to take Shannon home. Although he had showered at Eva's place, he could not bear the thought of taking her to bed after having bedded someone else just hours ago. Thus, there was an awkward moment when he had to make excuses to his girlfriend as to why he would not spend the night.

As he expected, Shannon thought he was joking. He had never turned down an opportunity for sex.

"Very funny, Stanley. Where's the camera?" Shannon made as if to look around for hidden cameras beneath the car's visors, the center console, and in the backseat. They still sat in his car parked in the parking lot at her apartment complex.

Her little smirk told him that she thought he was teasing. This was a first in their relationship and it pained him to turn her down. She enjoyed sex as much as he did, although she was sweetly shy when they first got together. She was beautiful and he could feel his traitorous body beginning a counter argument when she slid her hand up his chest.

He reached up and stilled her hand as he leaned forward to kiss her lightly on her mouth.

He got out and came around and opened her door for her. They held hands as they walked up the stairs toward her apartment door. Dark had fallen. The apartment complex was well lit, but nothing completely corralled darkness. Stanley slowed his pace as they reached her floor and moved along the open walkway to her door. He had a strange sense of claustrophobia even though he could feel the evening spring breeze move over his skin. He let go of Shannon's hand and grasped the railing. The darkness closed in as it pressed against some invisible veil just inches away from him and waited for him to step away from a light source. Fear took him in its grip. He barely restrained himself from vocalizing an actual whimper.

The darkness seemed a consuming manifested being just beyond the circle of light around the apartment building. His car was parked in a well-shadowed spot, beneath a tree, just beyond the stairs and the nearest light source.

"Stanley …" He thought he heard his name carried to him from the hungry shadows waiting around his car.

"Stanley …" the voice whispered to him, but was overlapped by a sweet, dulcet tone.

"Stanley," Shannon's voice jolted him out of his frightened reverie. He jumped.

She had pulled her apartment keys from her purse and they dangled from her fingers as she stopped mid-way toward unlocking her apartment door. She was half turned back toward him. She was a good four feet from him.

He gave his head a shake and felt silly. His earlier sense of fear gone and almost forgotten. *How long did I space out? Why was I scared?*

"Stanley, are you okay?" Shannon's alarm showed in her voice as well as her expression.

His answering laughed sounded self-conscious and confused to his own ears. "I'm not sure. I just guess I had a little dizzy spell like some little old lady or something. I'm fine … Maybe I had one too many beers at the restaurant. I feel fine now, I promise."

"You've been weird all evening. Is there more going on at work that you're stressing about? You can tell me, you know," she said as she unlocked the door and then juggled her keys and purse as they moved into the dark apartment. Stanley had a moment – the barest breath – of remembered fear until Shannon turned on the lights.

"No," he answered after he regained his wits. "There's only the usual bullshit going on at work, nothing else."

She put her purse and keys on the dining room table that stood as the great divide between the living room area and the bar that opened to the kitchen area. The kitchen window was on the area that faced away from the front and back streetlights and he noticed the window was very dark. He averted his gaze and moved over to the window to close the blinds. He could not quite shake a sense of being exposed ... watched.

He felt his phone vibrate in his pocket. He barely managed not to jump like a nervous cat. He needed to leave.

"Hey, I need to get going. I hate it, but I can't stay tonight," he said as he moved to put his arms around her.

She stepped back and would not let him pull her closer for the good-bye hug he intended. She looked worried as her dark eyes roamed his face.

"This is the first time you haven't spent the night since our fourth date. Are *we* okay?" She asked. Her voice was warm, but he detected the slightest tremor of anxiety riding along the words like an oil slick across a crystalline lake.

He pulled her close and hugged her. He kissed her hair and then leaned back to cup her face in his hands. "Yes, baby. *We* are fine. That is one thing I can promise you. I just really am stressed out and tired. It is not you."

She studied him silently for a long moment before she relented. "Okay, then. I trust you this time, but you act like this again and you can expect to be thoroughly deposed," she said, laughing. This time her voice sounded more stable. She chose to believe him.

She wrapped her arms around his neck and pulled him down to kiss him. He allowed her to tempt him for a few rapturous moments of the Thai-tinged softness of her mouth. He finally, reluctantly, pulled away and bid her good-night.

As he stepped across the threshold of her apartment and into the night, he looked back at her. He did not know why, but her anxious brown eyes haunted him as she continued to stare at him until her closed door separated her from his view.

He descended the stairs and did not have a relapse of his earlier fear until he reached the third from the last riser. He stopped cold.

The sense of being watched expanded. The stairway ended about ten feet before the end of the building. The sidewalk continued past the building to the common sidewalk running along a row of trees planted in a landscaped rectangle between the sidewalk and the parking lot. His car was parked directly beneath one of the trees, about fifteen yards away, the furthest spot from the wall mounted light.

Stanley became steadily convinced that someone waited for him just around the corner of the building. His would-be assailant waited – tensed like a predator about to pounce – in the shadows just outside the light. He was suddenly certain of it. He could *feel* its presence.

He waited, statue still, and listened with a primal concentration. He heard the scratch of feet walking down the sidewalk -- but too far off to be his attacker. He heard traffic sounds that made up the ever-present breath of a large city. He heard a bottle roll across the parking lot and he heard the breeze as it exhaled through the leaves of the nearest trees.

He was about six feet tall. He was in good physical condition. He worked out on a regular basis. Only the rare people who saw him undressed knew he was lean and well-muscled. He also knew how to fight. He would not be an easy target.

So, why am I so scared shitless to walk from this staircase to my car? Why am I so fucking scared of walking past the edge of the building? He wondered.

He was scared and pissed at being scared. It was unreasonable, illogical and out of character for him.

Yet, it was still true.

In his grown man's heart, the little five-year-old boy surfaced to tell him that if he turned off the bedroom light, ran three steps and leapt as far as he could, he would make it to the bed without the boogie man's scaly arm reaching out from under the bed to snag one of his ankles and drag him off to a place too terrifying to name. That little boy now told him to run across the grass, away from the building before he reached the end, forgetting the human-directed sidewalk path, and sprint directly to his car.

He pulled out his keys and worked up his courage and descended the last two steps to the sidewalk.

He took a deep breath and ran to his right, into the grass and away from the building in a path parallel to his car, and then he bolted for the car -- unlocking and starting it remotely as he ran. He felt a moment of triumph as he wrenched the door open and dived into the driver's seat. He slammed the door shut and locked himself in.

He could now clearly see the shadowed side of the building and could not make out any would-be attacker. All Stanley could see was the swirl of a low fog that had begun to spread from around the building and past the lower steps where he had just been.

The fog was thick and aggressive. He shivered as he watched it.

It had been a long and strange day. He backed out of the parking space and headed home.

*****

Shannon was mildly worried. Normally, she was not the insecure type, but Stanley's strange behavior shook her a little with its sudden appearance.

They had dated for almost a year and he still kept it almost formal between them. She appreciated the respect, but she wanted to move the relationship to the next level of commitment.

Move the relationship to the next level? Really? If I were to say that's what I wanted to do, I'm sure he would run as far away as he could. She thought as she plopped down on her couch. She turned on the 11 o'clock news. Charles Kellerman reported the murder of a liquor store owner just before breaking away to the "cutest puppy pic of the day" right before the commercial.

She knew she was sulking, but could not seem to stop. She wanted Stanley's warmth and his attention in bed. She found it sweet that he had no clue just how good he was in bed. Thinking about him made her shiver in the best way possible.

She got up and went to her bedroom to change into the shorts and tank she normally slept in, then she went to the freezer and pulled out a nice, creamy frozen treat by her friends Ben & Jerry. She sat on the couch and ate her ice cream from the container as she watched the odd array of news and distracted her thoughts from going to insecure places.

Things with Stanley were going to be fine. She knew this. He said he would take her to Disney World, after all. He seemed like he meant it.

With that thought, along with her ice cream, Shannon began to feel a little better.

*****

They enjoyed the meal that gained a new family member. But … there was a better meal coming if they were patient. Time was different for Them. They traveled and learned and tasted what the world had to offer. Finally, when the Hunger began its relentless gnaw, They knew it was time to return to the place and time best suited for the hunt.

The previous taste of Stanley, mixed with Eva's sweet longing for him, made him worth acquiring. He was strong-willed. He would not have normally been a Siren to call Them, but then his infidelity with Eva showed Them he had at least enough of what They required to obtain him. The hunt was as sweet as the meal. He would be Theirs forever.

They returned to the time and place best suited to locating their prey. They hid within the woods behind Eva's house. Their many voices – layer upon layer – whispered like static to one another until the best strategy was decided. They waited until sunset and then located him going into a building.

He stopped at the railing and stared out at Them as if he saw Them even though they veiled themselves as darkness until they wanted to be seen. Moments later, when full dark fell, they waited around the corner from the stairs as a test.

He hesitated. He sensed Them. He bolted away from the building and moved swiftly to his car. They unveiled Themselves and prowled low to the ground. They allowed him to see Them as They moved across the ground. He drove away quickly.

He's sensitive to us. Interesting. Oooo .... But We love a challenge.

They moved through the night and waited outside his condo.

*****

Stanley arrived back at his home in the Paradise Cove Condominiums. The development was in a beautifully landscaped gated community. He always felt a twinge of pride when he got past the gate and drove through the gently winding streets. The streets were lined with custom sidewalks that meandered through frequent landscaped stops. Those stops were inviting park-like oases with ornate street lights and park benches. There were also larger areas that featured swimming pools, tennis courts, or parks with picnic tables, a small lake, and a playground for children. The condo complex was made up of several four-story buildings laid out in a symmetry that only a manmade development could attain.

He parked his car and hesitated only a moment as he experienced a return of his earlier fear before walking up the stairs to this third-floor condo. He bought the condo four years ago at a great price because it was still being developed. Now, it was a highly desired neighborhood and the property value had skyrocketed.

He put his keys in a glass bowl once he entered his home and began his usual rituals. He went into his bedroom to change into shorts and a tee-shirt then grabbed a beer from the fridge before he stepped out onto the balcony, picking up his cell phone, on the way. He settled into one of the patio chairs and sat his beer on the elaborate mosaic-tile-topped table. He now noted he had in fact missed three calls from Eva.

There were three voicemail messages.

He hit the button to play the messages and took a swig of his beer as he listened. The first one was just ten seconds of static. The second message held the same static, but he could swear he heard sounds beneath the static. He could not decide what they were.

Finally, the third message began with the same eerie static but after fifteen seconds he clearly heard a voice – Eva's voice --say his name. Her tone sounded almost confused and the last syllable of his name she spoke with a slight upward note as if she spoke his name as a question.

Then the voicemail ended.

He grunted to himself, "Humph ..." and listened to all three messages again.

He checked his photo gallery and noted the dirty pictures were still gone. Deleted. He relaxed a little. The background picture remained the one of him and Shannon.

He was tempted to call Eva back, but then decided it is not a good idea. *You are so chicken shit*, he chided himself. He changed his mind and called. He wasn't sure what to think when the call rang several times before going to voicemail. He decided not leave a message. After he had hung up, he gazed across the complex, lost in thought.

One of his favorite things to do was sit on his balcony because of the view. Across the street that wound its way on this side of his condo complex, was a landscaped cove with a large, well-lit swimming pool. The pool was surrounded by trees and shrubs so as to give the sense of an oasis. A sidewalk ran between the pool and the road. There was another sidewalk on his side of the street and then a large "wooded" area complete with a Koi pond and a couple of park benches closer to his balcony. It was not natural. It was designed to inspire, but he loved it anyway.

Suddenly, in his peripheral vision, he saw something in the landscaped wooded area closest to his balcony.

It was a fog bank.

It was an anomalous swirling gray-black accumulation of thick fog that appeared nowhere else except the wooded patch nearest his balcony. He could not see the shrubs, the park bench, nor the flowers where the fog bank hovered. He leaned forward in his chair and put his arms up on his balcony. There was a female figure within it. She was barely visible – just a slightly darker figure that manage to remain static within the constantly moving fog.

He could not make out any specific facial features, nor could he see eyes, but the upturned tilt of her head made it appear that she was watching him. He did not dare blink or move. The feeling of being watched was so powerful that he was uncomfortable and vaguely unsettled. He decided it was time to cut his balcony time short and call it a night.

*****

That night, Stanley had his first wet dream since puberty.

In the dream, he approached Eva's house. Bright light poured from every window and there were the unmistakably raucous sounds indicative of a party. He approached the door, raised his hand to knock, but the door swung open as if he had been announced.

He was greeted by a large, well-muscled man wearing a black suit and a long-nosed, green and gold Venetian mask. He could not determine an eye color through the shadowed holes of the mask, but the man's mouth was thin-lipped and smiling.

"She's been waiting for you," he said, teasingly. With his hand, he signaled for him to follow. Stanley trailed the man through a crowd of people all dressed for Eva's masquerade. There was music. Somewhere there was a full live orchestra (although he could not imagine where it could be in Eva's little house), and it played a classical piece full of power and drama. The percussion and brass thrummed through his insides. There were moments when the unexpected haunting lifts of a violin made his head spin. He became disoriented.

He found himself standing at the open French doors to Eva's back patio. Only there was no patio. A complete flat blackness stared back at him. He knew if he stepped past the threshold, he would be consumed by the darkness, or simply drop and fall forever.

He was frozen with fear until a soft hand on his shoulder broke up the staring game of chicken he played with the darkness. He turned to see Eva. She wore nothing but a short, red satin robe and a white feathered mask that covered the top half of her face. It was lined with glittering rhinestones. Her dark hair spilled down her shoulders in thick, loose curls.

"Stanley, it's so good to see you. I thought you'd never come back."

She took his hand and led him away from the open door. She tugged him through the living room, which took some effort.

The crowd was dense and rowdy. Men and women pushed against him, touched him, he felt lips kiss him and tongues tasted the back of his neck as he moved through.

It seemed it took a very long time to get to her bedroom. She pulled him in and shut the door. It was quieter in her room. The bed was still messed from where they had lain hours before. *Had it really only been a few hours?* Stanley felt the sense of confusion swallow him again.

"A few hours for you, my love ... but much longer for me. So much longer than you would believe. I have missed you," she said. Eva's eyes were dark behind her mask, but he caught the shine of her eyes from the lamp by the bed.

"Dance with me," she whispered and slid her arms around him.

Until that moment, he had not noticed he wore the same clothes he had changed into after he had gotten home – his tank top and shorts. It seemed he and Eva were sorely underdressed compared to the crowd outside her bedroom.

His arms went around her of their own accord. *It's just a dream, dumbass. Don't worry about Shannon. This isn't real.*

Eva began to sway to the rhythm set by the muffled orchestra. He soon joined her. He felt her hands play at his back and he allowed his hands to roam her backside through the sensual fabric. He moved his hands up to her face and he tipped her chin up. She appeared more than willing for his kiss.

He hesitated as he gazed into her eyes through the mask. The shadowed eyes looked back at him regarded him with an intensity that made him uneasy.

"I am only allowed to go so far until you make your choice. You must come to me, Stanley. Kiss me ... please. I want nothing more," she whispered.

He felt her heat and her energy pull at him.

"It's just a dream," he whispered. He sunk his fingers deeper into her thick chestnut curls and lowered his mouth to hers. The connection of their mouths had an electric effect. He felt a jolt through him. He had an aching erection and a fierce need to tend to it.

As if sensing his need, Eva pressed herself closer to him as their mouths moved together – tasting, teasing. His tongue probed the silky softness of her mouth. She groaned and reached to lift his shirt. They broke contact for just a moment as she helped him pull it off.

He loved the feel of her soft hands roaming freely over the bare skin of his chest. She was far more aggressive than the one time they had been together in reality. She nipped at his hardened nipples and he shivered. He moved to open her robe, but she stilled his hands. She smiled up at him and reached over and opened her closet door.

"I have a surprise for you … five minutes in Heaven," she whispered as she tugged on his arm to lead him into the closet. Something did not seem right. He hesitated, but she was surprisingly strong and caught him off balance. He stumbled into the closet with her. She closed the door and all light was sealed off.

He began to panic. The darkness had been waiting for him. He sensed her with him in the dark. He felt her hands. The desire was primal. His entire existence was solely located between his legs at the moment. He felt her pull down his shorts. He had not bothered with underwear when he got home.

His erection sprang free of its soft barrier and he felt her hands working over him. Touching him in unfamiliar ways that made him gasp. He could not see her. He could not see anything, but some latent sixth sense knew when she lowered herself down. He groaned when he suddenly felt her take him into her mouth. He reached down and buried his hands in her hair.

She suckled him roughly and did strange and wonderful things with her tongue. It did not take long until he was overwhelmed with a long, shuddering climax. She did not pull away. As if his issue were an offering of honey, she drank him with soft satisfied sounds. His own vocal expression of ecstasy was loud and coarse.

The lights came on and he was blinded.

Her closet was suddenly the size of a cavern illuminated by an unnaturally bright bare bulb in the center of it. He squinted as his eyes adjusted to the light. He became aware of the presence of others in the closet with them. The whole of Eva's party guests had somehow crowded into the closet and stood shoulder to shoulder in a tight circle around him and Eva. They all stared in a feverish but utterly complete silence. He stood naked in their circle with his shorts around his ankles, having his dick post-coital lick-cleaned by Eva, who went about the task with no self-consciousness whatsoever.

When she finished, she stood and looked up at him. A strangely triumphant smile on her lips. "Now ... you are mine."

"What? *No!*" Stanley felt it was imperative suddenly that she understood this was not the case.

Her smile widened to reveal a mouth crowded with needle-like teeth.

"Mine," she insisted as she moved toward him.

Stanley cried out and tried to back away, but his feet got tangled in his shorts and he fell backward ... and fell ... and fell ...

******

Stanley awoke as he hit the carpet in his living room. He banged his head on the leg of his coffee table as he sat up. He looked around – completely disoriented. He had gone to bed in his own bedroom.

How the hell did I end up here? He was naked except for his shorts which were around his ankles and probably the reason he fell, but he could not remember getting up.

He did not remember leaving his bed.

He shook his head to clear it. He recalled the erotic dream and looked down at his penis. The dream had been so erotic and real ... he knew the orgasm had been genuine, but he saw no evidence of it on his member or his thighs. He remembered the thorough tongue-bath Eva had given him in the dream. His penis stirred. He got up off the floor and pulled up his shorts before anything could get started.

He told himself again it was just a dream.

He moved from the living room toward the kitchen area where his table overlooked a pretty window and yet another landscaped walkway below.

He froze. Lying on his table was single white feather -- a long, narrow feather like the ones on Eva's mask in the dream. He stared at the feather for a long time. He simply could not fathom what it meant.

He slowly approached the table and picked up the feather. It was real. He rolled the base of it between his fingers, then he walked over to his kitchen trash, stepped on the pedal that raised the lid and threw the feather away. He preceded with his routine to make his morning coffee as he blended his morning fruit/protein smoothie.

Later, he took a hot shower and let the water soothe him. He felt strangely safe in that humid, cocooned environment. He realized he had a headache as he dried off and he reminded himself to take a couple of pain relievers before he left for work.

He thought about work. How was he going to handle seeing Eva this morning? He knew it was a potentially awkward situation. He used a hairdryer to clear the steam off of his bathroom mirror as he thought about what to say to her. As he looked at his reflection, he went very still. For the third time that morning, he had a strange moment of confusion.

He stared at his reflection. The man looking back at him was a subtly improved version. His silver eyes were more intense and the lashes framing them darker. His skin was perfectly clear and his face looked leaner as did the rest of his body. He leaned closer and rubbed a hand over his hair. It seemed a little thicker than it had been. None of the changes were all that noticeable individually, but collectively he could tell a marked – however small – difference in his appearance.

He had a moment of fear. *Real* fear.

However, it was only a moment.

At some point, Stanley made a conscious decision that everything he had experienced this morning was simply not possible. He shook off his fear and finished getting ready for work, feeling much better.

*****

Eva was not at her desk when Stanley arrived at work. This was not unusual as he always arrived at least an hour before the paralegal team he supervised. He sat down at his desk, fired up his computer, and was soon lost in the mountain of work he had to dive into at the beginning of his work week.

It was 11 a.m. before he surfaced from his workload. Eva's cubicle was across the hall from his. When he was seated at his desk, he could normally see her at her computer. He looked over and saw she wasn't at her desk. At first, he thought she had stepped away, but then he noticed the little lamp on her desk was off and her computer screen was black. There was an undisturbed quality to her workspace that bothered him.

He got up and walked down the cubicles that banked the area across from him until he came to the next one. Heather Watanabe looked up from her computer as he stepped into view.

"Good morning, Stanley," Heather's heavy Southern accent was charmingly disconcerting paired with her exotic Asian features. At the moment, her dark eyes roamed him appreciatively. "Did you do something different? You look extra spiffy today."

"No, nothing different ... I just decided to bathe in awesomeness this morning," he joked, then changed the subject. "Have you seen Eva Shelby today?"

Heather appeared to think about it for a moment. "I've been pretty busy with Monday stuff but, now that you mention it I haven't seen her at all this morning." Heather gasped. "In fact, I *know* she hasn't been here because she is always the one that makes the coffee. So, *that's* why there was no coffee this morning!"

"Thanks, Heather," he said. He wandered around and made the same casual inquiry of a few of the other paralegals and received the same answer.

Stanley did not care for the feeling that crept over him. He could not define it, except that it was a sense of disquiet. When he returned to his desk, he did the next logical thing any supervisor would do – he attempted to call her.

The call went to voicemail. He was suddenly taken back to the dream from the night before when he heard her cheery, throaty drawl. *I have a surprise for you ... five minutes in Heaven.* He shivered and was relieved her voicemail was a standard, "Hi, this is Eva. Leave me a message and I will get back to you as soon as I can. Have a great day!"

He hesitated a moment before he fumbled through a message, "Hey, Eva. This is Stanley. Can you give us a call here at the office? You are scheduled to work today. Thanks ... bye."

Stanley had used the work phone to call. He hung up and studied her desk across the hall. In the past five years he had worked with her, she was consistently responsible. She had never before been a no call-no show.

He had to admit he was worried and by the end of the day. He was *really* worried. After work, from the privacy of his car, he called her from his cell phone and got her voicemail again.

He didn't realize he was going to run by her house to check on her until he pulled into her driveway.

*****

Eva lived in an older, quiet suburb – very different than the modern oasis in the center of urbanity where he resided. In real estate magazines, her house would be described as a small brick bungalow. She had a tiny, covered front stoop, but a nice-sized back patio. The house only had one bedroom, but it was a very large bedroom. It was a good size for someone living alone or a couple with no children.

Being an older neighborhood, one tended to get more for one's money. As such, the lots were bigger. Her front yard was a good size, but he knew her back yard was huge.

He gazed at the house as he sat in the driveway, parked behind her car, and he tried to decide if it was appropriate that he was here. Finally, he decided his concern outweighed his appropriateness scale. He exited the car and walked up to her front door.

He could not shake the sense of déjà vu he experienced as he knocked on her front door. He looked around as he waited for an answer. Despite the fact her car was in the driveway, he felt a sense of emptiness about the house. A ghost town sort of sensation.

When he did not receive an answer to his second knock, he decided to walk around to the fenced back yard. He opened the gate and went around to her back patio.

Something made him break into gooseflesh and the hair bristled along the back of his neck as he approached the patio.

Eva's French doors were wide open.

He stopped for a moment before he came around and faced the doors at the only entrance up to her back patio without climbing a raised, waist-high brick wall. He stepped up a couple of stairs. The prickling along the back of his neck increased. He turned and looked around the back yard. There was a wooded area at the end of the lot. The sun had dropped in the sky but had not set yet. The shadows were deep and long. He could not see far into the wooded area, but he became convinced he was being watched.

He shook it off and faced the open doors. *I have a surprise for you ... five minutes in Heaven.* His imagination had a good time at his expense.

"Eva?" he called out. If she was home, he did not want to scare her.

He stepped closer and called her name again, this time a little bit louder.

He carefully stepped through the doorway and looked around. He was first assaulted by some unpleasant scents. He smelled human waste, urine, and the coppery scent of blood. One step further into the room and he could see the hardwood floor was smeared with half dried fluids and waste. He barely managed to keep from stepping in it.

His gorge rose. He fought the urge to throw up.

"Eva!" he shouted without shame this time, but he already knew he would not receive an answer. The unnatural stillness about the house told him all he needed to know.

He looked around from where he stood. The wall to the kitchen was on his left. On the pass-through to the kitchen, a shelf had been built. Stanley noticed a dozen roses in a crystal vase sat on the shelf.

The roses had not been there twenty-four hours ago when he was last with Eva.

He looked past the roses and into the kitchen and he could see two wine glasses sitting on the ceramic tile-topped island.

He recognized the glasses as being the ones they had drank from the night before. He briefly considered washing the glasses and putting them away but realized he would probably only leave more evidence and make himself look guilty. He'd watched enough episodes of crime shows to know not to touch anything. He also noticed Eva's cell phone was on the counter next to the roses.

A million things he was not proud of ran through his head. He was scared of how it would look once it was discovered he was probably the last person to see her alive. He didn't want to lose Shannon. He did not want to lose his job if it were discovered he had been sexually involved with someone under his authority. He hated that some panicked, unchivalrous thoughts made him want to cut and run and pretend he had never been there.

However, despite a moment of weakness, he liked to believe he was – at his heart – a good man. He held on to that thought and got a grip on his emotions. After a few deep, calming breaths. He decided it was time to suck it up and do the right thing.

Stanley stepped back out into the fresh air on Eva's patio and called the police.

*****

Once the police arrived, he found himself in the midst of a storm of activity. He sat outside at Eva's café table on the patio and answered a myriad of repetitive questions delivered by a detective named Todd Barnes.

The forensics techs came and gathered up evidence in bags from the drying fluids on the floor. Stanley did not care for the way the cops stared at him. He wanted to cry. He was caught between guilt and shame for what he had done by sleeping with her (and keeping that part of the evening to himself), and genuine grief for a woman for whom he cared.

At some point, a tall, dark-haired man arrived on the scene. He was dressed just as the movies always depicted F.B.I. agents – in a suit and wearing dark glasses pushed up on top of his head. He approached and introduced himself by the name of Special Agent Clive Clay to Detective Barnes. They shook hands and Barnes introduced Stanley to the agent. The detective had icy blue eyes that were almost feverishly intense.

He was taller than Stanley, but he was also just plain ... big. Broad-shouldered and barrel-chested, the hand he extended to Stanley was huge, long-fingered and strong as he took Stanley's for a handshake. Stanley was properly intimidated and did not care for being the focus of the man's gaze. He strongly suspected there was not much Agent Clay missed.

"Mr. Crump, can you walk me through the events that led up to you deciding you needed to call the police," Agent Clay said.

Stanley almost inquired as to why he had to go through this again, but something in Clay's eyes, made him wisely halt his protest before it was uttered.

Stanley took a deep breath, "I came over yesterday evening – sometime before dark – to return a book that she had loaned me for my girlfriend, Shannon. Eva is a big fan girl of vampire stories and Shannon has gotten hooked on them, too.

"I gave her the book and she invited me in for a glass of wine and she said she would be happy to pick out some more books that she thought Shannon would enjoy. We sat on the couch, sipped wine, and talked about books for a little while and then I excused myself to leave because I was late picking up my girlfriend for dinner," Stanley explained.

"What time was that?" Clay asked. Stanley realized that Clay didn't write his notes down like the local police.

"The sun had set, but there was still some daylight. I guess it was around six or so," he guessed.

Agent Clay asked Detective Barnes if he got the name of the restaurant. Barnes gave him the name of the Thai place Stanley had provided earlier.

"Okay, so you left her around six-ish ... was there anything different about her? Did she seem nervous? Upset?" Clay asked.

"No, not at all. She seemed fine, but she did mention that she had a secret admirer who had been leaving her roses," Stanley said. Suddenly, he recalled that she had brought a single rose to work the Friday before. He told the two authorities about it. "She said she had a 'secret admirer' who had left it for her."

"Did she say anything else about this 'secret admirer?'" The intensity level in his blue eyes actually heightened, although Stanley would not have believed it was possible.

"No, but she did say something about having a new boyfriend last night. I don't know if the secret admirer and the new boyfriend are the same person," Stanley answered.

Clay considered Stanley for a long moment. Stanley had to fight to keep from squirming under the man's gaze. When the agent's eyes abruptly glanced away and toward the open French doors, he felt a powerful sense of relief, as if he had been removed from a fire.

"I'm ready to walk the scene now," the agent advised as he began to walk away.

Detective Barnes looked both intimidated and annoyed. He glanced briefly at Stanley and said, "Don't leave town. Remain available, we may have more questions later. I think you can go for now."

Then the detective left to catch up with the FBI agent. Stanley was happy to get out of there.

He knew one thing for certain – he hoped to never again be on the receiving end of one of Agent Clive Clay's searching stares. The man's intensity was frightening.

*****

Clive Clay had dismissed Stanley Crump as a suspect for the moment. He knew Crump was hiding something, but he did not think he had anything to do Eva Shelby's disappearance. Something within Crump's silver eyes hinted at guilt, fear, and grief.

After fifteen years in the Bureau, Clive's sense of people was seldom wrong. He was a human lie detector. If he had to guess, he figured Crump had done more than talk books with Eva last night and he was having guilt over it because he has a girlfriend he obviously gave a shit about.

Clive stepped through the French doors and was slapped with the distinctive odor of bodily fluids and waste. He watched Forensics gather samples off the floor, dust for prints and check for DNA on the wine glasses situated on the kitchen counter, and take lots of photos of the house.

Detective Barnes, now irritated that Clive had walked away, caught up with him. "Agent Clay," the young detective began, "Are you sure about letting Stanley Crump just leave?"

Clive kept assessing the room. He spoke to the nearest Forensics tech, "Look under the couch and any furniture nearby. You might find something there," he said. The tech gave the agent a nod before Clive turned to answer Barnes' question, "Yep, I'm sure. He was hiding something, but it wasn't anything to do with Eva Shelby's disappearance."

He moved into the kitchen, trailed by Barnes. He saw nothing out of the ordinary except the two glasses on the counter, both with small drops of wine dried to a tacky consistency in the bottom. He moved his gaze from the glasses to the roses sitting on the pass-through shelf. He watched a tech bag the cell phone. They would check that back at the office.

The agent moved from the kitchen, through the living room, and into the bedroom. The room had a distinctive female décor. The bed covers were tossed back and rumpled. He sniffed the air like a hound. He turned back to Barnes, who had followed him into the room.

"Get Forensics to check the sheets. I am willing to bet that we're going to find semen and we will need DNA," he said.

Barnes looked at him for a moment, perhaps a little resentfully, before he disappeared. He returned a moment later with a tech who went about the process of determining if there was anything on the sheets.

"Looks like we have semen," said the tech, holding a light over the sheets.

"We should probably call Crump back to get a DNA sample from him," said Barnes.

Clive shook his head. "No, let's take a kit and go by his work first thing tomorrow. He may remember more by then. Plus, he'll have some time to stew in his guilt. I think he'll admit to whatever it is he's hiding by tomorrow. He won't be able to stand it anymore."

Barnes opened his mouth to say something else, but was interrupted by a scream from the Forensics tech. Suddenly, a large, crazy creature bolted from under the bed with a loud and frightening yowl, and he promptly attached himself to Clive's leg.

"What the hell was that?" Barnes said.

Clive reached down to soothe a fat, gray cat. He checked the cat's tag. "Apparently, Ms. Shelby had a pet. Detective Barnes meet Chester."

Barnes looked at the cat. The cat ignored Barnes and took to rubbing on Clive's leg. Clive sneezed. He was horribly allergic to cats.

He sneezed again and gazed down at the traumatized feline. "Great ... I'm allergic to the only witness to what happened to Eva Shelby. Oh, and he doesn't speak human."

*****

Clive took the fat hungry cat back to his hotel room with him. He stopped off briefly to buy a couple of small dishes, cat food, a litter box, cat litter, and some non-drowsy allergy medicine.

He had a cat for a few years as a child, he recalled. His mother bathed the cat once a week to keep Clive's allergies at bay. Getting rid of the cat was not an option because Clive refused to give him up. He would sneeze all night cuddled up with the feline he named Sherlock, after his fictional hero.

Apparently, Sherlock thought the baths were a method of torture because, after two years of weekly baths, Sherlock shot out the front door one evening when he had an opening and never came back. Clive had not had a cat since then.

Presently, he put Chester down on the floor in the room's bathroom where he set up a litter box.

"I don't know why I am babysitting you, furball. It's not like you can help with this investigation," Clive muttered as he filled a bowl with water and put it on the floor near the television.

"Meow," Chester said as he used the litter box and proceeded to follow Clive closely because he seemed to intuit that he was about to be fed.

Clive sneezed as he filled a dish with food and put it down. He had to laugh as Chester immediately attacked the bowl with gusto.

He settled down on one of the beds while the cat ate. He sneezed again and pulled out the allergy meds and popped a pill, washing it down with a bottled water on the nightstand between the two double beds.

His cell phone rang. It was Detective Barnes. "You were right, Agent Clay. Forensics found what appears to be a distal phalange bone under the couch, just a couple feet from where all the fluids and stuff were found. They have to test it for DNA, but it's a pretty good bet that it's Eva Shelby's," he said.

They had found the tip of one of Eva Shelby's fingers. Clive was suddenly very tired. "Yeah, it will be hers. You won't find anything else," he said with a weary sigh. He rubbed a hand over his face.

"Have you seen this before? Is this a *serial killer*?"

Clive pretended he did not notice the hint of excitement in Barnes' voice. "Something like that. I guess 'serial killer' is as good a description as any."

They made plans to meet up at the law office where Stanley Crump worked the next morning.

After he had ended the call, Clive laid back on the bed and fell into an exhausted slumber. He had not slept in 24 hours. He had been following this – whatever the hell it was – thing from Oklahoma. Before that, Utah, Arizona and California were the first. He wasn't sure how it chose victims and that frustrated him. If he could figure it out, then he might be able to predict where it would go.

He awoke from a nightmare two hours later, gasping for breath, and suppressing the urge to scream. In the dream, he saw Ashley, his wife … He watched the fog drifted around her foot, snagged it and drug her away from him and pulled her beneath the car. It was an extremely narrow space, but the fog quickly covered her and pulled her beneath. He watched as the mass of swirling fog quickly flattened and it drifted off, leaving only a pile of clothes, bodily waste, and fluids.

He screamed her name as he awoke sitting upright in bed.

It took him a long time to calm down. The nightmares wouldn't stop. He was too late to save his Ashley. He was too late to save Eva or any of the others so far, but he hoped he would be able to figure out and save the next victim.

*****

Stanley decided not to enjoy his usual beer and deep thoughts out on his balcony. Memories of the woman in the fog bank had ruined his evening Zen. Instead, he had a couple of beers and watched television with no real memory of what he had viewed. He ignored a couple of missed calls from Shannon. He didn't know how to tell her about Eva's disappearance and he was still processing it, so he just had a beer and avoided it all until he was ready.

He crawled into bed wearing just his boxers around 10:30 p.m. and the dream began again. The man who wore the creepy long-nosed Venetian mask greeted him warmly, but he also seemed smug, somehow.

"I know something you don't know," the man sang to him, childishly.

"What do you know?" Stanley demanded.

"I'll never te-ell," the masked stranger sang, then indicated that Stanley enter the house.

Stanley pushed through the crowd of the masquerade attendees in Eva's house until he reached the French doors. The darkness moved just beyond the threshold of the open doors. It seemed to boil and black bubbles pushed inward past the threshold here and there. Something tried very hard to get in.

It was something he was pretty sure he did not want to see. He backed away from the doorway to avoid being touched by the blackness. He turned as he felt the soft tap on his shoulder. Eva was there wearing the same fancy white feathered Venetian mask and her short, red satin robe.

She smiled and reached out to take his hand and she led him through the dancing crowd that seemed to want to crush him with their bodies, touch him with their hands, or taste him with their tongues as he pushed his way through.

Finally, they were alone in her bedroom. He wanted this to go differently, but she remained so completely in control. He kissed her and suddenly realized he knew she enjoyed it because she allowed it. It would not have happened otherwise. She would not allow him to undress her. Again, she stopped his hands as he reached for the sash to her robe.

She opened the closet door.

"Don't you want five minutes in Heaven, Stanley?" She asked as she pulled him into the darkness within. He did not stumble this time. She closed the door and all light was sealed off.

After he had reoriented himself he fought back his panic. The dark waited for him. The darkness was so hungry.

He felt Eva's hands. He groaned as she gripped his thick erection in her talented hands. Her quicksilver fingers danced over the silken head and along his length. A sexual hunger like he had never known ignited within him.

The only sounds were his sharp intake of breath when she dropped down and took him into the soft heat of her mouth. He reached down and gripped her hair, this time he was not gentle and she moaned approvingly. He was fairly certain it did not take him the required "five minutes in Heaven" before he was seized with the biggest orgasm he had ever experienced. He threw his head back and cried out. She drank him in.

The bare light bulb was switched on and he blinked rapidly to overcome the initial blindness.

The whole of Eva's party guests stood shoulder to shoulder in a silent and tight circle around him and Eva.

When she finished suckling every drop he had to offer, she rose and kissed his bare chest, running her hands run over him covetously. "Mine," she whispered.

"No," Stanley stated with a calm confidence he did not feel. Eva's shadowed eyes were intense behind the mask. Her needle-toothed smile appeared.

The others in the cavern began to touch him and taste him. They were rough and there was nowhere their hands and mouths did not explore. He gasped in pleasure and pain.

He heard an impossible number of voices repeatedly whisper, "Mine, mine, mine...."

"No!" he shouted. In an impulsive move, he reached out and snatched off Eva's mask. Her face was missing from the nose up. There were just raw muscle and tendons oozing blood. Her blue eyes were wild. He screamed and tried to jump away, but the others prevented it.

"Why did you have to ruin it? Why aren't you just going with it like I did?" she screamed. Her beautiful mouth was an abomination below the ruin of the face above it. She reached for him with hands now bent into claws. He fought wildly as they pulled him down to the closet floor to tear him apart.

*****

Stanley woke screaming inside his closet.
Naked.
His partially turgid penis was in his hand.
At first, he continued to cry out as he was so completely disoriented and it was dark. He thought he was still in the dream until he felt his shoes beneath him and he bumped into the back wall and one of his suitcases tumbled down on him.
How the fuck did I get in here?
He crawled out on his hands and knees. His head pounded and he felt nauseated.
He was greeted by hundreds of white feathers littering his bedroom floor like a downy snowfall. The feathers stuck to his sweaty hands and legs.
What is happening to me? Is this what happened to Eva? This is impossible!
He slowly managed to attain a vertical position. He made it to the bathroom and turned on his shower and immediately felt a little better as he stepped under the hot spray of water. He remained there until sanity returned and he felt almost human again.

Stanley arrived at work right at seven a.m. He was on time, but for him this was late. Usually, he prided himself on being the early one. The supervisor who set a good example. He was normally at work by 6:45 a.m. each morning.

He logged into his computer and began compiling his daily reports in preparation for the usual 9 a.m. meeting with his supervising attorney, Mel Weathers. It was around 8 a.m., and he was processing the third of his five reports when he received a call from Mel Weathers' office.

He picked up the phone, "Hey, Mel. I'm working on the reports now. They should be ready for the 9 a.m. meeting with the partners."

Without any preamble, Mel said. "Stanley can you come to Conference Room 1, please?" His voice was quiet. Grave.

"Is something wrong?"

"Can you just come down here? It's important."

A stone fell heavy into the pit of his stomach. This was not good. He found a stopping place in his work and wandered down the hall. He passed Heather Watanabe's cubicle. She called out to him.

He turned and paused at the entrance. She had her head tilted to one side. "What are you doing different, Stan da' Man? I hope you don't think this is like ... sexual harassment or something, but you are looking *really* good and I want to know - what is your secret?"

Stanley chuckled and shrugged. "Clean living, I guess." He winked at her.

"Yeah ... riiiiight," she laughed and waved him off.

He made a pit stop in the men's room on the way to the Conference Room. He went to the sink and splashed cold water on his face. He grabbed some paper towels and patted his face dry and stared at his reflection in the mirror.

He was floored by what he saw.

His hair was thicker. His silver eyes gazed back at him with a mesmerizing intensity and his lashes were thick and dark – the envy of most women he knew. His face was ... *arresting* was the only word he could think of to describe it. There was a powerful radiance that exuded from everything from his laser-like gaze to the impish quirk of his sensual mouth.

A transformation, he realized. His next thought was a naked whisper – *Just like Eva's transformation.* He began to tremble. *What is the price of this transformation? Will I disappear next?*

He could feel fear riding toward him on a wild horse. He moved from its path. He felt ... too powerful to allow this to happen. He shook off the terror that waited like a vulture circling. He straightened his tie and went to his meeting.

His first impression upon entering the conference room was he had somehow made a wrong turn and ended up at a police station. Mel sat on one side of the conference table and Detective Todd Barnes and another detective sat across the table. It was an interrogation room setup. Mel indicated that he come and sit in the chair next to him across from the detectives.

As he moved toward the chair, Stanley suddenly noticed another man in the room – Agent Clive Clay loomed quietly in a corner watching the proceedings. The agent's icy eyes tracked his progress to the chair.

Once Stanley was settled, Mel said, "These detectives have come to speak to you further about Eva Shelby's disappearance."

Stanley looked from Mel to the police detectives. "I told you everything I know yesterday evening."

Barnes learned forward. "Mr. Crump, first let me introduce Detective Kyle Dawson. He's assisting with this case. I believe you remember Agent Clay." Barnes tilted his head in agent's direction.

Stanley nodded to the new detective and to Agent Clay.

"We have gathered samples from Ms. Shelby's house. We have contacted her family. There have been some new developments," Barnes continued. "One is that we did find part of a finger bone at the scene – which is now officially a crime scene – and given the condition of the scene and the fact that no one knows where she is, we have to assume foul play.

"Another development is that we discovered seminal fluid on Ms. Shelby's bed sheets. So, we would like to extend you an opportunity to cooperate. We have brought a swab kit. We would like a volunteer DNA sample from you. We would also like to ask you if there is anything about the nature of your relationship with Ms. Shelby that you would like to disclose before those results come back?" Barnes opened a notebook and picked up a pencil, prepared to take a statement.

Mel reached over and put a hand on Stanley's arm. "You don't have to answer that if you don't want to."

Barnes gave Mel a sharp look. "Are you his attorney?"

A veteran attorney, Mel was unruffled. "Does he *need* one?"

Barnes looked directly at Stanley. Stanley did not look away. "That depends on Mr. Crump."

Stanley patted Mel's hand. "It's okay.

He took a moment to compose his thoughts and get his emotions under control before he spoke. "I told you everything about the other night except for one thing – Eva and I had sex before I left. It was the first time. I can't even believe it happened, but it did. We had been drinking wine and talking about books. Eva was different than she had been ... flirty ... aggressive ... tempting.

"I don't know how to explain it. We had been good friends and co-workers ... there had been an unacknowledged attraction there for a long time, but I have been in an exclusive relationship for nearly a year. It was one of those things ... I didn't expect it to happen ... but it did. I am ashamed because I cheated on my girlfriend and because Eva is someone I directly supervise. It shouldn't have happened."

The detectives asked him rapid-fire questions, many of which repeated what he had told them the day before. They asked invasive questions about the sex – Was it rough? Was it consensual? Was there anything unusual? Stanley answered everything as honestly as he could. He felt like shit, but he answered honestly.

Agent Clay remained silent throughout the whole interrogation. He stood in the corner, leaning against the wall. His eyes never wavered from Stanley.

When Dawson and Barnes were finished, he finally spoke up.

"I just have a couple of questions ... one is about the 'secret admirer,' you said she talked about. Did you ever see any evidence of the admirer?"

Stanley thought about it. "She brought a rose to work Friday, she said it was from her secret admirer."

"Is that all you can remember about him? She never described him or said if she had set a date to go out with him or anything like that?"

After a moment, Stanley shook his head. "No, not that I can remember. All her references to him were really vague."

The agent strolled over to an empty chair on the other side of Dawson. He pulled it out and sat down closer. It was all the agent needed to do to be intimidating. "One more thing ... you said Ms. Shelby had been 'different' lately. What did you mean by that?"

"She wore her hair down at work – which she rarely ever did – and she just had that air about her ... you know ... that way a woman gets when she has a happy secret. Then ... the night I came by, she was so flirty and was not trying to hide it. She was never so bold before," Stanley explained.

The agent nodded slowly. "The night you were with her ... did you notice anything physically different?"

Stanley shifted in his seat and looked away. "There were little things ... but it sounds crazy."

"Indulge me," Clay said. The two detectives stared at the FBI agent, obviously puzzled.

"She looked ... better. She was always pretty in a 'smart girl' kind of way. But ... over the last couple of days she looked more radiant. She was ... beautiful ... just all of a sudden ... she was head-turning beautiful and sexy ..." Stanley trailed off as he tried to remember more. Suddenly, he remembered something. "There was one really weird thing ..."

"What was that?" The agent did not seem surprised by anything Stanley had said.

"I noticed it after we had finished having sex ... we were laying on the bed together afterward and I noticed a bunch of little bruises on her ... they were small bruises here and there, but they were all over her body. I asked her about them and she said she did not know where they came from. She said she had been sleepwalking lately. I remember that it worried me ... she promised me that she would see a doctor if it kept up."

The agent appeared satisfied. After the detectives performed the cheek swab for DNA analysis, the agent and the detectives left and Mel and Stanley lingered in the conference room a bit longer.

After a moment, Mel said, "Stanley, I want you to take a few days off."

Stanley opened his mouth to protest, but Mel interrupted him. "Your job is not in jeopardy – I don't think there's anything substantial that implicates any involvement in Eva's disappearance. Your reluctance to talk about your infidelity so as not to put your current relationship at risk was not your best decision, but it was understandable. The important thing is that now you have cooperated fully. However, this is a trauma and I insist that you take a couple of weeks of vacation time – effective immediately. God knows you've got that and more saved up."

"One week. I will take one week if it makes you happy," said Stanley.

Stanley left the conference room and went back to his desk to shut down his computer and gather up some things he wanted to take home with him. He slammed his laptop into travel bag as well as some files he had meant to catch up on. He was angry at this interruption in his life.

Interruption? You are such an incredible asshole! Eva has disappeared and is probably dead and you are upset at how much YOUR life has been interrupted. You whiney ass bitch!

Stanley was immediately penitent on the heels of his own self-chastisement. He left his office in humbler state of mind.

In the parking garage, he slowed his approach to his car as he saw Agent Clay leaning against a black SUV parked next to Stanley's car.

"Is there something else you needed, Agent Clay?" Stanley asked as he approached.

The agent walked up to him and handed him a business card. There was an additional number written on it in red ink. Stanley looked up from the card, eyebrows raised.

"That's my cell phone number. I just wanted to make sure you understand that this killer is very dangerous. I want you to call me if you think of anything that you remember that might have been suspicious ... I mean *anything*, no matter how crazy you think it sounds. Do you understand?"

Stanley nodded. The agent turned abruptly, got into his vehicle and left before Stanley could say a word.

*****

Stanley did not know what to do with himself when he got home. He was OCD about his job, he hated leaving with work undone. He got home and changed into workout clothes and headed to the workout room. He did more reps with more weight than he had ever done before. He used his frustration, his grief, and his anger over the whole situation as fuel for his workout. He did not tire until almost two hours later.

He returned to his condo to take a shower. He collapsed onto his bed afterward but jumped up abruptly when he realized he'd begun to doze off. He was afraid of what would happen if he fell asleep in the middle of the afternoon. He worried he might leap naked from his balcony or worse.

He had never felt so alone. He thought of Shannon and called her on impulse.

Her voice was throaty and sweet, "Well, hello stranger."

"Hey baby. I'm sorry I haven't called in a couple of days, but something terrible has happened. I have been dealing with a lot. Can I come over when you get off from work?"

"Sure ... but only if you bring beer and pizza," she said, teasingly.

He was never so glad she was the coolest woman he had ever known. "You got it."

He arrived around 5:45 p.m. with beer and a loaded pizza. Shannon had already changed into shorts and a tee-shirt – her at-home attire.

After they settled down at her kitchen table, he poured out everything – with the notable exception of his having had sex with Eva – to Shannon.

She listened intently ... stunned by the whole story. When he finished, she just stared at him. "I don't even know what to say ... this is horrifying. So ... they think she's dead?"

He nodded and took a good pull from his long neck. "Yes, that is the assumption. I was the last person to see her alive. I didn't have anything to do with it, but I feel guilty for some reason ... like a weird guilt by association. I was the one who called the police after I had gone to her house to check on her. Being a no call/no show at work was not at all like her and she didn't answer her phone."

Shannon reached out and touched his hand. "Was it awful? Her house, that is ..."

Shannon's touch ignited something within him. It awakened a powerful need – more powerful than he had ever experienced before.

In fact, so powerful that his voice sounded hoarse to his own ears as he answered, "Yes, it was awful, but not like you would expect. There were the smells ... the stuff on the floor – the police tell me it was all body fluids and shit. The worst thing was the silence. I don't know how to explain the feeling of 'emptiness' that was in the house. It reminded me of when my grandmother died."

He turned her hand over and began to caress the underside of her wrist as he spoke, "I was about ten years old. There were two moments from then that never left me. I was very close to my granny. She was so full of life. I don't ever remember her without a smile on her face until the day of the funeral. I walked up to the casket and I couldn't stop staring. She looked like she was asleep, but you knew she wasn't. It's like there was this vacuum of nothingness around her body. I had heard the expression that the human body is just a 'shell.' That's what it seemed like ... it was just an empty shell laying there. Granny was gone."

Her dark eyes were riveted to his face. Shannon's eyes were so dark brown, that in some lights, it was hard to see her pupils, but there was enough sunset light coming in through her windows that he could see her pupils had dilated.

She was fascinated by what he said, but he could also see the telltale beginning signs of arousal. He slid his hand around to the top of hers and drew little circles on her skin with his fingertips as he continued, "The second thing that stayed with me was when we went to Granny's house later after the funeral. There was family all over the house. We were all packed in there – dressed in black.

"I wandered away from the crowd and found myself standing in the doorway to Granny's bedroom. It was weird. There were people all over the house, but it was like everyone avoided this room. I walked in and climbed up onto her bed like I had done so many times in the past. This time there was a strange stillness about the room. It was like walking into a photograph. It had that same vacuum feeling – an abandoned shell. It was all wrong. Something important had been removed. Its life had been sucked out. That's what Eva's house reminded me of. That's what it felt like – it was too still – too silent ... like the life had been sucked out. I just knew something was very wrong so I called the police."

There was a long silence after he finished. He and Shannon just stared at one another. It seemed his need was like a disease that had infected her as well. For him, it was a raging fever. He and Shannon had always had amazing chemistry, but what he felt now was different. It would not be ignored. He still held her hand as he stood up and, without a word, pulled her to her feet and led her to the bedroom.

She offered no resistance, which was fortunate for them both because he was not sure if it would have mattered if she had ... and that realization frightened him.

Stanley was swiftly becoming a stranger to himself.

*****

Shannon had felt a growing sexual tension from the moment Stanley walked in the door. She didn't know if it was because she had so much pent up frustration after their last date – which ended with no sexual satisfaction – or if Stanley had just done something different to his appearance because he looked good. Really, *really* good.

He moved more fluidly and his face seemed leaner. His hair was thicker. It seemed crazy because she knew he was not a vain man. He would never have done anything to enhance his appearance except for his workouts, and that was for the purpose of health. His appearance was just an added benefit. She had learned early on in their relationship that he was a practical man.

However, this evening he was something else. His eyes were the most striking difference. Stanley always had beautiful silver eyes. However, now they had a practically preternatural glow. His intensity dial had been turned up.

Physically, her body did not want to resist. Her mind knew something was ... off. However, her body was digging the whole new sexy Stanley vibe he had going. Her libido wanted to dance to the new rhythm he laid down, so there was no thought of resistance where she could stop and ask questions.

She just allowed him to lead her to her bedroom.

Once in the bedroom, he pulled her arm and used the forward momentum of her body to catch her up against him. His silver gaze locked with hers. So intense were his eyes that it was almost a relief when he lowered them to look at her mouth. He lowered his mouth to tease her lips. He nipped at her bottom lip and teased her with light kisses until he settled his mouth on hers for a long and slow kiss that made her knees tremble.

She was already barefoot and Stanley broke the kiss to kick off his shoes. He had not worn socks. She had a full-length mirror in her room and he turned her away from him and toward the mirror. He looked into the eyes of her reflection. She watched him lift her hair and kiss the back of her neck. His tongue traced paths along her skin. She gasped and her eyes slid closed.

"Open your eyes and watch. I want you to watch me make love to you," Stanley murmured against her skin. There was a little bit of steel in his voice – just enough to promote his statement from the rank of a request to a direct sensual order.

He slid his hands down her waist until he reached the bottom of her tee shirt. He grasped the bottom and lifted it up and off over her head and tossed it to the floor. She looked at herself now in shorts and a lacy pink bra. His hands slid around and cupped her breasts over the bra. He planted small sweet kisses along her shoulder as his hands slid around and caressed her waist and abdomen. He caught the waistband of her shorts and pushed them down her thighs until they were at her feet. She stepped out and kicked them aside.

In the reflection, she watched his eyes drink in her curves in the matching pink bra and panties. His hands moved over her body. He used one hand to tilt her head to the side and he kissed the spot where her neck met her shoulder. She gasped softly and shivered with a need that was growing to match his.

With one hand, he held her honey-colored hair out of the way as he kissed her neck, and with his other hand he unfastened her bra. There was a sudden looseness. She trembled and watched as he brought both of his hands to the bra straps and drew them down her arms in agonizing slow motion. Her breasts finally sprung free and he completed the bra's journey and tossed it onto the floor with her other clothes.

"Look at you, Shannon," he murmured against her ear.

She watched his eyes wander over her breasts. She was heavy breasted almost to the point of being what her mama would call "busty." Once again, she watched his strong, masculine hands move in slow motion as they crept around from behind her to caress her waist and move upward to cup her bare breasts. He rolled her nipples between his fingers and kneaded her breasts. He began to roll and tug at each nipple alternately *almost* too hard – just hard enough to make her gasp in pleasure, not pain. She groaned and her head fell back against his chest. Her eyes slid closed.

"Open your eyes and watch ..." Stanley issued another sensual order and tweaked a nipple to get her attention.

Her eyes opened immediately and she raised her head to watch as his hand moved down her body to catch on the waistband of her panties. He tugged them down slowly, turning the act into a mesmerizing erotic show.

This was what she found so addicting with Stanley. His sensuality, his complete control and sexual creativity. He was a generous and exciting lover, but there was something more aggressive about him this evening. She watched as her femininity was slowly revealed. He stopped the descent of the panties halfway down her thighs and he used one of his feet to push her legs apart. From behind, he reached forward and easily slid his fingers into her.

She gasped and could not stop a whimper of pleasure from escaping. The image presented to her in the mirror only enhanced the experience. She stood naked with her panties halfway down her thighs while he worked his fingers between her legs.

He slid his other arm around her waist to support her because her knees gave way as she gasped and writhed against his moving hand. She felt his erection throbbing against her backside through his cargo shorts. She knew from previous experience with him, that he was going crazy, but he always had an almost unnatural level of restraint.

She felt the telltale beginning of an orgasm building and her impending release excited her, but he suddenly stopped.

"Please," she begged, breathlessly.

"Not yet, baby," he cajoled. "You know how this goes ... you also know I will make it worth the wait."

She whimpered, but she trusted him. He knew what he was doing. He turned her to face him and he pushed her panties the rest of the way down. She stepped out of them and kicked them away. He cupped her face in his hands and kissed her. She leaned into him and found the friction of her naked skin against his clothing to be intensely erotic.

His hands came down to roam her body as his tongue plundered her mouth. When the kiss finally ended, he gazed at her from beneath lowered eyelids with his laser-like silver eyes.

"Undress me," he commanded, softly.

She immediately pulled his shirt up and over his head. She gasped in surprise as his chest seemed to have become even more muscular than he had been before. She ran her hands over his skin in lust and wonder. She followed the work of her hands with kisses as she tasted his skin. She felt a sense of deep, feminine satisfaction when she felt him shiver in pleasure. She reached down and unfastened his shorts and quickly drew them down, along with his boxers. She did not have his patience.

He stepped out and kicked his discarded clothes away. He stopped her roaming hands to turn her back to the mirror. He pulled her tightly against him until she could feel his erection firmly pressed against the cleft between her buttocks. He moved one of his hands upward to toy with one of her breasts and nipple, while his other hand crept around the front and down between the folds of her womanhood to excite her to the point of near climax again.

When she was ready to beg him again, he turned her around and moved her toward the bed where he pushed her down and back. He pulled her to the edge of the bed where he pushed her legs apart and then lowered his mouth to her feminine folds. He used his fingers to press them apart – spreading them wide before his eyes – and then he used his tongue to make her scream. He had a mysterious motion he did with his tongue – a cross between suckling and flicking – she had never experienced any other man. He managed to bring her to orgasm twice on a small scale and finally a third time as a finale and she could not stop herself from screaming his name.

He was right. He always made it worth the wait.

Before she could come down completely, he whispered, "My turn."

He pulled her up roughly and lifted her bodily. He carried her to the wall at the end of the bed and lifted and braced her against it. She wrapped her legs around him and he brought her down on his shaft – filling her completely and forcefully. She moaned in surprise and pleasure. He had never done this before. She had never realized how strong he was until now. The wall braced her back and he set the rhythm with his hips and held her hips with his hands as if she weighed nothing.

She clung to his shoulders and he thrusted deeper until she could no longer tell where he ended and she began. She would not have thought it possible, but she could feel her fourth climax building and she knew he could feel it too. He waited – holding off his own release – until she was close then he pushed harder and their cries of passion mixed as they managed to climax within seconds of each other.

Later, they lay in each other's arms and tangled in bedsheets. She watched his expression as he drowsily contemplated her ceiling fan.

"What are you thinking?" she asked as she toyed with his hair. She lay on her side facing him as he laid on his back.

He looked at her then. His expression was utterly unreadable. His eyes were intense with an emotion she could not define. "I was thinking that I should have told you a long time ago that I love you. I've never said the words before ... but, it's true. Shannon, I love you. I've been in love with you since that first date when we took that selfie by the river walk."

Her hand froze in mid-motion. She had never wanted to push. She never asked him for anything, but she had been in love with Stanley Crump for quite some time. She had just been waiting to know how he felt. "I love you, too ... for a long time now."

He smiled then. She hoped she would never forget that moment. His smile was sheer bliss in the dimness of her bedroom. The sun had set but there was a little twilight indigo left in the gloaming and it seeped into her room from the between a slight part in her bedroom curtains. It bathed both of them in a shade of blue-gray.

They held each other and fell asleep with the contentedness of children.

*****

Stanley was dreaming again.

He wanted to roar in frustration as his feet felt compelled to move forward toward Eva's front door. There was a full-blown live orchestra – this time it played wildly thumping swing – somewhere within the tiny house.

He was disturbed by his utter awareness that he was dreaming, but apparently unable to stop it. He concentrated on his fist as he raised it to knock on the door. He tried to will his hand to drop and his body to turn from the door.

The door opened as if he had been announced and the man in the long-nosed Venetian mask welcomed him.

The man was naked except for the mask. Naked and obviously aroused.

Well, this is a new development, Stanley thought. He was afraid of where this was going.

"She's been waiting for you. We are all so glad you could make it," he said. He motioned for Stanley to enter.

Stanley fought the forward movement to cross the threshold, but his feet had a mind of their own. He moved straight ahead toward the patio doors. The blackness was violently pushing inward now and a hand formed out of the darkness and it reached into the house stopping just short of him. The fingers reached and curled … reached and curled.

Stanley was terrified his feet would take a notion and take that last step. Suddenly a tap on his shoulder made him turn away from the hungry dark.

Eva stood behind him. "I've missed you so much, Stanley."

She wore her red, silk robe and the white, feathered mask. He looked down at himself and realized he wore only his boxers. This time, he and Eva were overdressed for the occasion. The crowd of party guests were all naked except for the various Venetian masks they wore. The men all sported proud erections of one size or another and he could only assume the women were in their own state of arousal.

They reached for him as he walked the gauntlet of guests. Hands pulled at him. Body parts pressed against him, and mouths tasted his skin as he walked past. All of them cajoled and catcalled him as they attempted to pull him from Eva's hand, but she was stronger.

They were soon in Eva's bedroom with the rumpled bedclothes. Kissing her was more intense than in the previous dreams. His arousal was complete and maddening almost immediately. He wanted nothing more than to take right her there on the floor.

"Oh, Stanley ... It is soooooo worth the wait for five minutes in Heaven," Eva whispered as she stopped him from pulling her robe open. She opened the closet door and pulled him inside.

The darkness was complete and oppressive when she closed the door. Something was in the enclosed space with them. It moved lightly over his skin and he tingled everywhere it touched him. He felt Eva's hands on him. She was not gentle as she yanked his boxers down.

This time he did not leave them around his ankles, he stepped out of them and kicked them to the side. He felt her hands on him and she slid down his body and he felt her take him in her mouth. This time there was pain mixed with the pleasure as she nipped at him. He winced. Something about the nature of her aggression triggered his free will.

Desperately, he wanted her to suck him off, but almost as desperately he wanted to be awake and away from her. He was suddenly convinced this was not entirely a dream. He tried to pull away from her and she clamped down harder with her teeth. He cried out in pain and found his erection throbbed in response. It almost pushed him over the edge.

He began to struggle harder. He reached down, grasped her hair, and yanked hard in an attempt to pull her off of him. She hissed and other pairs of hands grabbed him in the dark. His hand was pulled from her hair and his arms were held straight out from his shoulders on each side.

Hands held his legs in place and Eva went to work biting and sucking. He tried to cry out but a hand grabbed his chin and a mouth began kissing him. His scream was muffled by the stranger's mouth. The unseen stranger's tongue explored his mouth and he fought harder, but still his body was only pushed closer to climax despite the pain of Eva's bites and the hands that held him so tightly as fingers dug into him.

Other hands began to explore him. One hand squeezed his testicles below Eva's working mouth and countless other hands roamed his body touching him everywhere and soon those hands were joined by mouths that tasted, sucked, and bit at him. He screamed against the mouth that still plundered his as he experienced a mind-shattering orgasm. His hips pumped against Eva's mouth and ...

... and ... he heard a voice calling to him. He tried to call back but the stranger's mouth still covered his. He fought harder and then he was suddenly released when the closet was filled with a blinding light and he was falling ....

*****

Shannon awoke. She had fallen asleep with Stanley curled at her back. His warmth was now missing. She reached behind her to feel for him. She sat up in bed when she realized he was gone.

She could not figure out what woke her at first until she heard the sound again. It was a strange muffled whimpering sound – like a wounded animal. In the darkness, she gasped to see a male figure at the end of her bed. She put her hands to her mouth and tried to remain quiet as her eyes adjusted to the darkness and she tried to make sense of what she was saw.

A nearby streetlight threw some illumination into her room, casting crazy shadows on the wall at the end of her bed as the light filtered through a tree outside her window, but there were other longer, darker shadows that streamed in across her room from the window.

The man at the end of the bed was still mostly in darkness as the light fell in front of him to paint the wall, but enough reflective light revealed the man was naked. He faced the wall – away from Shannon.

He twitched and she heard the whimpering noise again and she realized it came from the man. His arms were stretched straight out to each side. Trembling, she rose out of bed as silently as she could and moved back and down to the end down the bed. She clasped her hand tightly over her mouth to keep from screaming.

The whimpering, struggling man was Stanley. He stood spread-eagle but he was struggling and his limbs were intertwined with and held by long tendrils of shadow … gray/black shadow. His mouth was partially open but muffled – blocked by an ashen tentacle of shadow that moved around it.

It seemed some huge gray monster had him in its grip and was attempting to tear his arms off or strangle him. Her eyes moved down his torso and there were tendrils of these shadowy things moving all over him. Her gaze reached his hips and she saw his erection and she saw the largest pool of gray-black shadows formed into the shape of a kneeling woman. She was prostrate in front of Stanley with his erection thrust into her head where her mouth would be – if she had one. Stanley emitted a muffled scream and his hips began to thrust forward in the telltale signs of an orgasm. The shadow thing was taking in whatever he was pumping out. It was hard to tell in the dark. Stanley continued to struggle – it was obvious he was putting up a fight.

Shannon quietly backed up and flipped on the overhead light switch.

The room was brightly illuminated. It hurt her eyes and she had to shadow them from the sudden onslaught of light.

The shadow thing was a dark gray, from what she could tell through squinted eyes, and it screeched and hissed at her … one tentacle flashed forward, serpent-like, and pushed her against the wall next to the light switch. She hit the wall and the thing hissed again and morphed into a large, single gray mass that funneled itself into a single, thick tentacle that flowed out of her bedroom through the window, which had been opened just a crack. It left through the crack, flowing out like a tumultuous gray river.

Once released, Stanley fell limp as a rag doll to the floor.

Shannon ran to the window and slammed it all the way down and locked it. She made sure the curtains were closed and ran back and knelt on the floor by Stanley. He just laid there looking pale and bruised. There were small marks all over his body that she knew would probably turn into bruises by morning. His penis, now partially soft, was red. He had small punctures and tiny beads of blood welled up.

She shook his shoulders.

"Stanley!" she screamed.

He did not respond.

"Stanley!" She shook his shoulders harder. Now, she was crying as she shook him. "Please, Stanley! Wake up!"

He groaned and she was never so happy to see another human being's expression of pain in her entire life.

"Oh, thank you, God! Thank you, thank you, thank you!"

He groaned again and opened his eyes. He looked around and said, "What happened? What the fuck am I doing on the floor?"

It was music to Shannon's ears.

*****

Stanley awoke, disoriented and naked, on the floor at the food of Shannon's bed. Shannon was kneeling over, crying and hugging him. His body ached all over and his crotch felt like someone had taken a hot poker to it. He gently cupped his bleeding and swollen genitals, curled up in a ball, and cried, "Ohmygod, ohmygod, ohmygod ..."

After a few moments, Shannon's hysteria abated and she wiped her tears and assisted him off the floor. All he wanted to do was weep like a woman, but something told him that would not get him anywhere.

"What happened?" Shannon whispered. Something in the careful way she looked over his shoulder toward her bedroom window gave him the creeps. She did not want to be overheard.

"I really have no idea, but I think it is connected to what happened to Eva Shelby," he whispered back. "I have been having nightmares. I thought they were just dreams."

"They weren't just dreams. There was something in the bedroom earlier. I found it attacking you ...it was ... I think it was seducing you, but you were fighting it ... it was raping you, I guess."

"What did you see?" he asked as he stood and gathered his clothes. He gingerly began to get dressed as he listed to her description.

Shannon followed his lead and got up and began to dress as she explained the gray/shadow/tentacle thing that had him in its grip.

He felt the blood drain from his face and his knees gave way. He sat down on the edge of the bed and fought back more tears. It just wasn't manly.

He spoke quietly and in shame, "It's real and it's after me and I brought it here. Forgive me, Shannon. I didn't realize ..."

"This is crazy, Stanley! What was that?" She looked like she was ready to dismiss all that she had seen because it simply wasn't possible.

Stanley spotted his wallet on the floor. It had fallen out of his pocket. He picked it up and thumbed through and found Agent Clive Clay's business card.

"I don't think it's crazy and I think I know someone who can help," he said as he called the agent's number.

*****

It was just before the turncoat time of the night when FBI Agent Clive Clay arrived at the door to Shannon Beckman's apartment. It was the time of night where one can feel the night turning to morning, betraying its nature, even though the sun had yet to make her grand entrance.

In deference to the late hour (or early, depending on how one looked at it), his knock on the door was soft and it was greeted almost immediately by a lovely, leggy blonde with very dark, brown eyes. Not at all a bad sight for this time of day.

"You must be Agent Clay," she said quietly as she ushered him in. "I'm Shannon."

He reached out to shake her hand. He found her grip to be firm but trembling as her slender hand was swallowed whole by his. She put on a good poker face, but the handshake told him what her dark eyes would not.

She was much more afraid than she let on.

She led him across the room to the kitchen table situated between the living room and the entrance to a small kitchen. Stanley sat at the table with one of his legs propped up on an extra dining table chair. His shorts were unzipped and he had what appeared to be a bag of frozen peas on top of his crotch. Stanley's silver eyes practically glowed, but his face was pale and frightened. His hands shook and he wiped almost constantly at a silent flow of tears from his eyes.

Clive settled into a chair at the dining table and Shannon sat in the other empty chair. He looked from Stanley to Shannon and back.

"What happened?"

After a long pause, Stanley said, "It started with a feeling ... like I'm being watched. Then, the dreams started. The dreams are real. I don't know how else to say it. You think you are in one place dreaming, but it's really happening to your sleeping body ... It somehow gets in your head."

"What gets in your head?"

"The Fog ... the Fog Bank ..." Stanley almost broke down, it was obvious he worked hard to fight it.

Clive put his hands on the table. "How do you know it ... this fog ... gets in your head? Or that it is really doing things to you?"

Stanley pointed at his crotch and then held his arms out for Clive's perusal. "Because it left marks! Because my dick looks like someone used it for a pin cushion!"

As Clive examined the long, ropy bruises forming on Stanley's arms, Shannon spoke quietly.

"I saw it," she said.

Clive's startled gaze snapped to her face. She looked at Stanley's arms and then at not much at all, but sensing his regard, she met his eyes directly.

"I woke up and he was at the foot of the bed. At first, I couldn't understand what I was seeing ... I mean it didn't make sense. I walked to the end of the bed and there were these shadows ... he was being held and ... um ... sexually assaulted ... by these shadows. When I turned on the light, it was gray like a fog ... and it formed into one large tentacle and left out a crack beneath my window. I thought the window was locked ... but it wasn't," her voice hitched, but she did not cry.

"Is what happened to Eva going to happen to me?" Stanley asked. "Am I going to disappear? Is this thing after me? I know you know something ..."

Clive shook his head. "I don't know much. I know that this is all X-Files kind of shit. The first case that I know of began in a town in Southern California. I wasn't involved until the third disappearance. They have been calling it a 'serial killer,' but as you have seen that's a cover. It kills serially, but it's not some human we can profile and track. In my field, I have a great track record for catching bad guys, but this thing ..." he searched for the right explanation.

"I haven't been able to figure out all the connections between the victims. Some of them are opportunities and have an obvious and trackable connection to a previous victim, as in your case Mr. Crump. But ... Eva Shelby ... I can't figure out why she was chosen. The last victim was in Oklahoma and we've tried figuring out a connection, but we just can't. It has slowed some since Oklahoma – where three people disappeared that we know of --- but the disappearances are further apart. I think it means something, I just don't know what."

Clive sighed as he looked at Stanley. "I have to be honest with you, Mr. Crump. The bad news is that what is happening to you is what we have heard reports of before the victims disappear."

Stanley let out a slightly hysterical laugh. He raked his hands through his hair and leaned back for a moment. "Of course it is! That's my luck! What is the good news?"

"The good news is that I have never managed to speak to someone going through the dreams and the sleepwalking and the other phenomena that we have heard reported before a disappearance. So, I have to think that gives us an advantage that will keep the same thing from happening to you."

Stanley only appeared to be slightly comforted by this news. "So, what do we need to do?"

"The first thing is I need you to give me all the details ... I need to know everything that has happened to you and when it happened. You have already told me what you know about any precursors to Eva Shelby's disappearance."

Clive watched Stanley glance quickly over at Shannon, but was so fast that he was certain she didn't notice.

Stanley told them about the first thing was getting the mysterious phone calls with no answer. It seemed to Clive that Stanley was hiding something else about the phone calls, but he decided not to push it until he had a chance to speak with Stanley alone. Stanley moved on to recall the sense of being watched and how the fog showed up at Shannon's apartment complex and then later at Stanley's condo complex. He described the dreams – even though it was awkward and uncomfortable – he described everything as if he had never been with Eva Shelby as if it was just a random dream. He told about the single feather after the first dream and the sea of feathers after the other. He ended with what had happened earlier.

Shannon had been watching Stanley's face a little too closely after he began to describe the dreams. Tears flowed down her face. Clive had a bad feeling about what was to come.

"Stanley ... I am going to only ask you this one time and you better be honest with me. There's just something about the way you described the dreams ... did you sleep with her that last night you were over there?"

Stanley went pale and looked away from her. A war played across his features – shame, anger, fear – Clive expected he would deny it. To his credit, Stanley told the truth.

"Yes." His expression was utterly defeated.

Shannon jumped up suddenly from her chair. "You asshole! You lousy piece of shit! You weren't kidding when you said you brought it here! You said you loved me! Was that a lie? How long have you been sleeping with her?"

Stanley raised his hands in supplication. "It was the first and only time, I promise. I do love you, Shannon. I don't know what happened ... she was different ... It caught me off guard. I failed you ... I ...I ..." his voice trailed off as if he knew nothing he said would be enough to make up for the huge transgression.

Shannon picked up a towel that had been laying on the table and threw it at him. He caught it and just sat there looking completely miserable.

"Stop!" Clive shouted. They both stopped and looked at him.

"None of this matters now. Shannon, if that thing got a taste of your DNA off of Stanley, you could be next. Stanley, it's already courting you so we need to stick together. Take turns sleeping and put our heads together until we get this figured out and save both of your lives. After that ... once we get rid of this thing, then you can fight it out."

Shannon crossed her arms and leaned against the wall.

Stanley took the semi-frozen peas out of his shorts, zipped up and stood. "It doesn't matter Agent Clay. I've lost her already and I know it. I deserve whatever happens to me. I need to go."

Stanley headed for the door and Shannon called after him. "Oh, right! Go do something even more stupid now! You need to stay here, Stanley."

Clive stood and used a hand to silence her. She quieted and wiped the tears from her eyes. Stanley had opened the door and stood with it slightly ajar. He looked back as if he might reconsider.

"She's right, Stanley. Don't do something stupid because you're feeling guilty and emotional right now."

Stanley opened his mouth to answer but whatever he was about to say was cut off by a sharp scream from Shannon. A large gray tentacle of fog had slipped in through the crack in the door.

A lot happened very quickly.

Stanley attempted to slam the door shut and step back from the doorway, but more of the fog moved in. The door visibly bounced from the force of the fog. The tentacle wrapped itself around Stanley's waist and halted his attempt to run.

Clive ran to the door and pushed as hard as he could in an attempt to close the door, but the fog was a force he had not expected. He could not budge the door and a second tentacle flowed in and swatted him away like a horse swatting away a fly. Clive was knocked off his feet and onto his back. He slid about four feet and crashed into the chair he had occupied only moments before.

More tentacles flowed into the room – living smoke. They encircled Stanley's limbs. Another large one encircled his chest and began to crush it. Clive could hear Stanley's ribs crack. Stanley opened his mouth to scream when another tendril of fog shot through the door and into his mouth the tendril divided and entered his ears, his nostrils, his eyes and more flowed into the room and slid beneath his clothes. Stanley's body began to thrash and twitch.

Shannon screamed and was halfway to Stanley when Clive regained his senses and grabbed her ankle and pulled her foot from beneath her. She hit the floor screaming. Some instinct drove Clive and he pulled her by her legs to him until he could get a good grip on her.

She fought him like a wild cat. She wanted to get to Stanley. Clive covered her mouth and wrapped his arms and legs around her. He had to silence and restrain her.

"Shut up! Shannon, he's already gone! Do not draw its attention or we're gone, too!"

Her muffled screams against his hand ceased after a moment. He covered her eyes from the horror in front of them. The fog was dissolving Stanley. His twitching slowed. His face slowly caved in and melted into the collar of his shirt. The bulk beneath the clothes began to do the same.

The monster was quick and efficient. The whole grisly process took less than five minutes until Stanley Crump was not more than a messy pile of clothes on the floor.

Shannon trembled in Clive's arms from repressed sobs and screams.

When it finished feeding, the Fog Bank hovered for a moment. Clive remained very still. It moved about the room almost snuffling like an animal. It came very close to Clive's head. Shannon also went very still.

After what seemed an eternity, the Fog Bank slowly retreated and all of its bulk flowed back out of the room and out the door. Clive waited a moment then he released Shannon, gained his feet, and rushed to the door to slam it shut and lock it.

Shannon sat up, pulled her knees to chest, and buried her face. She rocked and keened. Clive stared down at the mess. Bodily fluids and waste covered Stanley's clothes. There was nothing else left.

Finally, he pulled Shannon to her feet. She didn't resist. She did not ask questions when he asked her to pack clothes for a couple of days.

"We can't stay here," he explained, though she robotically obeyed

He worked quickly to make a plan.

*****

Shannon averted her eyes as she and Agent Clay walked gingerly around Stanley's clothes and slipped out the front door. She watched the sky lighten just before the break of dawn. The sun was about to chase the darkness away.

She carefully thought about nothing. She did not want to replay what she had seen. Agent Clay had managed a tremendous mercy when he covered her eyes, but she had seen enough and she heard it all. The bones breaking ... the gurgles ... the wet sounds. Now, she enjoyed her carefully cultivated insulating numbness.

Stanley was gone.

She could not make that fact seem real. Not for the life of her.

Agent Clay spent some time on the phone with Detective Barnes as he drove outside of town to the motel where he had rented a room. She heard him speak as if he were a television at home when she was otherwise occupied – it was just background noise.

"I'm taking Ms. Beckman into protective custody. You can come by and question her later, after you have done all you need to do at the scene. Yes, she was hysterical. I could not get any answers out of her yet, but I thought it was a good idea to get her away from there for her safety."

Stanley was gone.

They arrived at the motel and Agent Clay directed her to the other bed in the room. He seemed to prefer the one nearest the window and door. She was okay with that. He was a very large and fiercely protective barrier between her and danger.

A gray ball of fur padded into the room.

"Ms. Beckman, meet Chester," the agent introduced her to the cat.

She reached down to pet him and he rubbed his face against her hand. "Hi, Chester."

"Chester has been through a lot, too," Clay said as he sat down on the bed with a sigh.

After a moment, she sat on the opposite bed and faced him. "What are we going to do now?"

The agent pinched the bridge of his nose and briefly closed his ice-blue eyes. He looked very tired. Finally, he looked at her. "I honestly don't know. I think right now we play it by the book for the locals. There's no way anyone is going to believe the truth. In the meantime, I have to keep you safe and we need to learn more about this killer. Knowledge is always power."

There did not seem to be anything to say to that so Shannon nodded. She took off her sandals, pulled back the covers, and got into bed fully dressed.

Almost immediately, she fell into a deep and mercifully dreamless sleep.

*****

The Fog Bank drifted back into the woods behind Eva Shelby's home. Stanley could see everything with new eyes. Eva and The Others showed him the ropes. He was raw power but he needed to eat.

We need to seek another siren.

He had a new family to feed. They roamed the city seeking the call of the Sirens that would pull them in with their need.

We can feed that need and then they can feed Us and increase Our number.

Suddenly, they stopped and branched out, feeling the air.

There's a storm coming. We need to take shelter but when it is over we will find another family member to sacrifice its mortality to become part of Us.

With that thought, they found a hole that led to a rabbit burrow that opened into a cave.

The Fog Bank rested and plotted.

Stanley enjoyed his new awareness, but some part of him felt the need to keep a precious name from the rest of them. The one he loved. He refused to even think her name.

He did not want their attention to be turned to her.

He did not want their taste to be tuned to her scent.

He did not want her to become their next Siren.

FOG BANK
PART III
Seeking the Siren

FOG BANK III

SEEKING THE SIREN

Cheveyo rode his horse hard through the night to arrive at the barren and isolated crater. Dawn painted the Arizona sky with the pastels that gave him a sense of beauty and power in a way most people of the modern age no longer understood.

The dreams had become urgent. They began four days previously. The Ancestors visited him and told him to come to this place to see for himself. He looked down into the crater now as he stood on top of the ridge that served as the lip of the crater. He drew strength from the dawn as he patiently waited for natural light to creep its way forward to warm him and his stallion.

If there had been anyone to observe him there, they would have thought he was a native statue, carved from the rock on which he and the horse stood. When there was light enough, he guided the horse down the steep wall of the crater, picking the way carefully across dry brush, loose rock, and dangerous crevices.

He reached the bottom to discover what he had feared.

The time had come they had all dreaded for centuries. He would have to go back home and pull together what few elders were left who would remember what to do.

The crack in the earth that had been sealed for so long was now a black seam that ran almost the full length of the half-mile crater. The edges of the fissure had pulled apart and the gap was at least 100 feet across and the edges crumbled inward. Hundreds upon hundreds of dead crows littered the area closest to the crevice. He gingerly moved around the black feathered corpses. The sight of it all made him go cold despite the rapidly increasing temperature of the rising sun.

Cheveyo was a man in his prime – his mid-thirties – and he was strong, but this sight made even him tremble. He silently turned his stallion around and began the trek back out of the crater. This time he urged the horse a bit faster, despite the need for care. They could waste no time. He dreaded the days ahead. He wondered how many people had already died to feed it. He already formed the words in his mind. The words no one from his tribe had uttered in centuries.

The desert demon was loose again. It was time to summon the Shadow Warriors.

*****

A clap of thunder violently yanked Shannon from her slumber and she awoke in a strange place and in a strange bed. There was an unfamiliar man asleep in an identical bed next to her. The beds were separated by a generic nightstand with a plain lamp, phone, and alarm clock and charging cell phones.

Another clap of thunder shook the room. She sat up and fought the panic that threatened to rise like gorge from a turbulent stomach. She could not remember where she was or how she got there.

A fat, gray ball of fur leapt up onto the bed and she gasped.

"*Meow.*"

She let out a deep sigh of relief as her memory flooded back. Grief, death, and terror was what she remembered.

Stanley is dead.

This was the third day since Stanley died and she still wasn't ready to wrap her mind around it or to remember what happened two nights before. She feared remembering might just loosen the few bolts that still held her sanity together. Instead, she reached out and pulled the big cat onto her lap. He snuggled against her and stretched his paws forward to knead the sheets.

"Good morning, Chester. How are you?" she whispered.

He looked up at her with an enigmatic golden gaze. "*Meow.*"

She was not sure what she expected, but it made her smile briefly – a momentary flash of sunlight in a storm of emotions that matched the turbulent weather outside.

"I see you and Chester have bonded. He seems to jump on you the minute you're awake every morning," said a male voice from the motel room's other bed.

She looked over to see a pair of startling blue eyes looking at her. "Good morning, Agent Clay. I thought you were sleeping."

"I'm a light sleeper," he said as he rose from the bed. The FBI agent, who had undoubtedly saved her life, stretched. It was quite a show. He was a very large man – at least six foot six by her estimation and built like a lumber jack. He had slept in a tee-shirt and sweat pants. Although fully clothed, the agent's sleep attire seemed too intimate to her. She cleared her throat and looked back down at the cat. Her long, honey-colored hair fell forward to shield her blushed cheeks.

The agent's cell phone rang from the nightstand between the beds. He unplugged it from the charger and answered.

"Agent Clay."

The room was so quiet Shannon could hear the tinny voice coming through the cell, but could not make out the words. The agent listened and ran one of his big hands through his sleep-tousled black hair. She used the opportunity to move Chester from her lap and slip out of bed to get a head start on use of the bathroom.

She grabbed her quickly packed bag and quietly closed the bathroom door. In a few moments, she stood beneath a hot shower and used the roaring water to muffle the grieving sobs that wracked her.

She now understood the meaning of the phrase that something was "weighing heavily" on one's heart and mind. Her head felt too heavy to lift and her heart seemed to be a lead weight in her chest. She leaned her forehead against the shower stall's wall. Stanley hadn't just died like an old man during a pleasant sleep. No, he had been killed ... slaughtered.

Eaten, her sadistic mind corrected. She fought not to remember. Thankfully, Agent Clay had grabbed her and covered her eyes to prevent her from watching Stanley's horrifying death by the ... whatever it was ... the entity ... the ... fog, but she still heard everything. She heard the awful wet choking gurgles during his last attempts to cry out before his vocal chords were gone and she heard the sounds of his struggles. Afterward, she would never forget the sight of what was left.

The whole scene of terror, pain, and death kept replaying itself inside her head. Last night before she fell asleep, she told Agent Clay about how she could not stop hearing the sounds or remembering what she saw. She just wanted it to stop running like a marathon horror flick through her head. He told her that it was PTSD – she had just suffered a terrible trauma and an even worse loss and it would take time to heal.

Healing seemed a distant dream as one reality haunted her – *Stanley is dead*. The man she loved – her lover, her friend – no longer existed.

She turned her attention to the shower and she scrubbed her skin pink as if she attempted to remove the memories along with any skin cells that might hold the taint of his death.

When she finally emerged from the bathroom, scrubbed and dressed, Agent Clay was gone. She saw a note on the nightstand, like a parting token from a temporary lover after a night of passion.

Ms. Beckman,
I have gone out for a run. I will be back in about 40 minutes. You have my number if you need anything.

- C

She could not believe his dedication. He ran faithfully every morning, even during such terrible weather. As if to punctuate her thoughts, lightning lit even the heavy commercial curtains, followed shortly by another clap of thunder than shook the building.

She was ready to go grab some breakfast by the time he returned. He was soaking wet in his shorts and tee-shirt. With her umbrella on her shoulder, she told him she was about to go walk down to the motel's diner and get some breakfast. He grabbed her arm as she passed him on her way to the door.

"Not a good idea," he said.

"This thing doesn't seem to want to attack during the day, Agent Clay. I think I'm safe for now."

After a moment's hesitation, he let go. "I'll join you in 15."

The stormy day matched the emptiness and violent grief she suffered within. She opened her umbrella and strolled the length of the motel toward the inn's restaurant. The rain came down at a hard slant, wetting her jeans. The rain was cold and the storm had dropped the normally moderate spring temperatures to a slight chill reminiscent of winter. She stopped short as a she noticed a fog rose from a nearby field. Her heart pounded and she fumbled in her pocket for her cell phone to call Agent Clay.

Her trembling fingers found her phone until she realized it wasn't fog she saw, but a mere mist rising from the warm ground. She had not realized how frightened she was until she put her phone back into her pocket and realized her legs were shaky and weak. She hurried to the restaurant and found a booth far from the door.

Her heart rate slowed to a more normal pace as she ordered a cup of coffee from an older woman with dyed red hair and a nametag that announced she was "Dottie." Shannon perused the plastic covered menu for a while. Her appetite was almost non-existent, but she thought the French toast sounded like something she could eat. Stanley's favorite breakfast was French toast. She forced herself not to think. She distracted her thoughts by looking around the restaurant and focusing on details – the waitress uniforms, the varied customers, the yellow-topped Formica tables that appeared retro-looking until one noticed the yellow was faded by wear – the look was actually old and not contrived. Shannon decided it made her like the little restaurant even more. She was sick of eating in new places made to look old.

The large windows lining the diner, alerted her to Agent Clay's arrival before he entered. He was an imposing figure who drew attention as he moved – he was large and wearing a rather funereal black suit. His black hair was still well from the shower. His expression was solemn and his eyes intense. Shannon watched Dottie's eyes track him appreciatively to the table where she sat. He slid into the seat opposite her in the booth.

Dottie's glance was not the only female attention Clay drew. Shannon had not thought of Agent Clay as attractive before. She simply had not noticed – he was her protector, a G-man, someone with authority; whose intensity was sometimes frightening. She had only peripherally even noticed he was male. She thought about Stanley with his ordinary, but clean cut good looks, his lean build, and his sharp, silver gaze. Stanley's looks were subtle and he would easily be overlooked at first. Agent Clay was a different matter, now that Shannon covertly studied his features over the top of her menu. His features were angular, even chiseled. He had an almost swarthy coloring, but his blue eyes peered out from beneath thick, dark brows like chips of ice. She found herself surprised to realize he was handsome.

Inwardly, she found the fact of Agent Clay's good looks to be matter of trivia -- interesting but nothing more.

Agent Clay also ordered coffee and they both placed their food orders. While they waited, he presented some news.

"Detective Barnes wants me to bring you in for questioning about what happened to Stanley Crump."

She felt her stomach clench. "Is that necessary? He came by the hotel a few hours afterward. I thought that was all the questioning I would get."

The agent gave her a look such as parent would give a child who had asked a stupid question. "Of course it's necessary. You didn't tell them anything. You were barely coherent. I've put them off long enough. We will need to get the story straight, but I think it's time you spoke to the local authorities and got it over with."

"So, what's our story again?"

He sighed, but his expression gave little away. She hated the fact that he was so hard to read. She suspected, judging by his dedication to duty, that a man like him would be torn between going by the book and doing what had to be done in the face of impossible circumstances. Circumstances in this case being a vampiric, man-eating fog monster. The absurdity of her own mental description almost made her laugh out loud.

However, as she gazed at the agent's intense and forbidding expression, she decided laughing out loud at their situation was probably not a good idea at the moment.

"You know the story, Ms. Beckman. We've been over it many times the past two days."

She nodded silently. Thankfully, Dottie came to the table at that moment to take their order.

Their meal ended all too soon and they were at the police station.

*****

Todd Barnes could tell Shannon Beckman had never been inside a police station before. The brown-eyed woman with the long legs and long, honey-colored hair, ogled everything. Her wide-eyed gaze took in the people waiting up front, the security doors, and the front desk. F.B.I. Agent Clive Clay was his normal, large and imposing self. His startling blue eyes gave away nothing and he never moved more than a few feet from the woman's side. Agent Clay had called ahead and Todd met them in front to take them back to the interrogation room.

Detective Kyle Dawson was waiting for them in the room. He was already seated, but rose briefly – as any Southern gentleman would do – for a lady like Shannon Beckman.

Agent Clay assisted her with her chair. Todd and Kyle sat on one side of the table and Shannon and Clive sat on the other.

Shannon was dressed in a pair of jeans, but also wore a crisp white blouse unbuttoned just enough to make life interesting, but not so much that there would be any doubt that she was classy. She wore a simple silver tennis bracelet and a pair of small silver hoop earrings – nothing fancy. She wore a simple black blazer over the blouse. Agent Clay, wore his usual black suit.

Hell, now I feel underdressed, Todd thought as they all settled in. He and Kyle were dressed in jeans and tee-shirts.

Looking at Shannon, his next thought was: *What man on Earth would cheat on a woman like that?* It made him wonder what kind of spell Eva Shelby had woven that would have made Stanley stray. He had been at Stanley Crump's interrogation and saw genuine confusion and regret in the man's demeanor. Now, it appeared that Crump's infidelity may had led to his demise.

"First, let me say, that this meeting is just to get your statement about what happened two nights ago when Stanley Crump disappeared from your apartment. We do know that Eva Shelby had disappeared in a similar manner about two days prior to that. Evidence found at both scenes has led us to the conclusion that they are both victims of homicide. So, your account of what happened that night could be crucial to catching this killer. Every detail, no matter how small, is important. Do you understand?"

The young woman nodded.

In the old days, he would have asked her to state her cooperation aloud, but now these statements were recorded digitally as video – so body language could be seen as clearly as words could be heard.

He began by running through a course of basic information – her name, address, and phone number; place of employment, and her relationship to the victim.

"He is- er ... *was* my boyfriend. We have been dating for almost a year," she said quietly.

"For the record, Ms. Beckman, please state the events that occurred – leading up to and including Mr. Crump's disappearance – to the best of your recollection on the night in question." Todd had a notepad handy to jot down things he would want to go over with her after she finished.

Before she began, she nervously glanced over at Agent Clay. They shared a quick look between them and he nodded to her, obviously encouraging her to speak.

"Go ahead, Ms. Beckman. Tell them what you told me," he said.

Todd was surprised to pick up a note of gentle protectiveness in the agent's tone. He knew that could be dangerous if the agent allowed his sympathy for the lovely young woman to cloud his judgement.

The agent had a calming effect on Shannon. She straightened her shoulders and cleared her throat.

"I knew something was going on with Stanley when he was late for our date the previous Sunday night. I thought maybe he was wanting to pull back from our relationship ... he was distant and distracted. We went out to eat at our favorite Thai place and he got a call on his cell phone and wanted to leave right after that. We went back to my place and things were different. He normally would spend the night with me on Sunday nights, but this time he said he was really tired and had to get up early. He had never done that before since our third or fourth date," she said, and then paused as she eyed the pitcher in the center of the table.

It was water and she requested a drink. Todd poured her a cup. Her hand only trembled slightly as she took a few sips before she continued.

"I did not hear from him after he left that night. I heard nothing from him Monday and most of Tuesday. You have to understand that this was not normal. He usually texted me or called me throughout the day. We were pretty close," she stopped again. Tears had cropped up ... she took a moment to regain her composure. Todd saw raw, genuine grief.

She pulled herself together and continued. "He called me late Tuesday afternoon and asked if he could come over when I got off from work. He apologized that he had not contacted me in a couple of days, but he was going through some stuff. I told him he could come over if he brought beer and pizza." She let out a little laugh at the memory.

Todd and Kyle both chuckled with her. Everyone knew beer and pizza was the way into anyone's heart. Agent Clay looked grim and impassive – per usual.

"While we ate," Shannon continued, "he told me about how Eva had not shown up for work Monday and that he'd had a bad feeling. He told me about what he found when he went to her house ... the silence ... the ... the stillness. The smell. He said he felt guilty even though he didn't have anything to do with her disappearance. He said it was like a guilt by association thing."

Shannon was silent for a long moment. A blush lit her cheeks and Todd could guess at what she was about describe next.

"Go on, Ms. Beckman," he prodded quietly.

"I don't know if it was the emotions of the moment but ... we ended up in my bedroom. We made love ... it was one of the most intense experiences. There was something different about him ... he was stronger ... more sensual ... more demanding ... I don't know what it was, but it was ... um ... amazing."

She paused and took another drink of water and then a deep breath as she fortified herself. Todd knew that the big moment was coming.

"We fell asleep and I woke up when Stanley was tossing and turning and talking. He sounded terrified. I woke him up and told him he was having a nightmare. He scared me to death ... we fell asleep again and at some point, Stanley must have gotten out of bed, because that is the next thing I remember ... hearing him ... screaming from the living room ... I ran into the living room and there was just enough light from the open walkway outside my front door so that I could see the door was open about halfway ... Stanley was ... he was melting ... it was like ... I can't tell you what it was like. I have never seen anything like that ... the sounds ... stopped ... I went down on my knees screaming and screaming ... I thought I would lose my mind! That's when Agent Clay showed up ... he pushed open the door and saw ... he saw what was left of Stanley and he came over to me and covered my eyes and got me to calm down ... I don't remember a lot after that ... until later in the day ... it was almost morning, not light out yet, but not far from it ..."

Todd and Kyle asked her more questions to clarify as much as they could.

They then turned the questions to Agent Clay. To clarify details in the report he had already filed.

Todd looked at the agent. Clive Clay met his gaze directly. The man's gaze was unnerving. Todd resented Clay's superior attitude. If he were honest with himself, he probably would admit there were personal reasons that would not reflect well on him and added to the real reasons for his resentment of Clay. One thing he did know with certainty, that he had met many people with Clay's intensity and far too many of them had been unbalanced. He wondered about the agent. Thus far, Clive Clay had been nothing but eerily efficient – his experience and instincts had been spot on from the beginning.

"In your report Agent Clay, you said Mr. Crump had called you in the middle of the night. How did he know your direct cell number?"

"I had given it to him after the interrogation at his workplace. I told him to call me if he remembered any extra details."

Although Todd could not see anything untoward about the agent giving his personal cell number to Stanley, he had a strong feeling there was a world of information the agent was withholding.

Todd continued, "So ... he called you and what did he say?"

Agent Clay signed, but repeated his story, "He said he was scared. He said he had been seeing things – a fog – and he thought someone was stalking him. He was scared ... terrified. Almost hysterical. He said he was at his girlfriend's apartment and asked me to come right away. When I got there ... I found a lot of human bodily fluids and a pile of clothes just inside the front door and Ms. Beckman was screaming -- wrapped in a sheet -- kneeling in the doorway between her bedroom and the living room. I made sure the area was secure. There was no one else there, so I went to calm Ms. Beckman. I called the local police and took Ms. Beckman into protective custody. She had to be walked through the most basic of tasks, including packing items to leave her residence."

There were no major holes in Agent Clay's story. It was what it was.

However, as the whole thing drew to a close, Todd could not shake a sense that there was far more going on. He wondered if he would ever know what really happened.

*****

Stanley's sight was multidirectional. He could see all directions at once as he had access to all the minds within The Fog. His first remembered awareness, after the terror and pain of his physical death, was looking down at his clothes on the floor of Shannon's apartment, smeared with blood, fecal matter, urine, and various, unidentifiable bits of himself. He moved his gaze from that horrific sight and saw the large federal agent lying on the floor with Shannon. The agent had pulled her against his body and was protectively curled around her. He had a hand over her eyes. They were lying very still.

The Fog crept closer ... the consciousness divided briefly – some were still hungry for more, but ultimately the rest knew the situation was not ideal. The meal would be bitter as neither the woman, nor the agent, were putting out the delicious needs of a Siren. He drew close to Shannon and reached out to touch her., but an opaque, gray tentacle-like protrusion moved toward her instead of his hand ... and he began screaming within his own mind.

The shock was too much. He blanked everything out for a while until later when he became aware of the cave. They were deep within a limestone cave and he could not see much except darkness. He began to realize there were many minds that made up The Fog. He was being trained to think in terms of "We" and not "I." "I" was not part of Their vocabulary.

Once Their eyes adjusted to the dark, he could sense the stone walls all around. They were deep within the cave. Resting and waiting. He could sense their irritation at his failure to come immediately on board. He was fully aware and possessed all of his memories. He was now a being of a pure – but shared – consciousness. His new existence grated against his strong sense of individuality. He could not do anything physically without the group – the "family."

He ached for Shannon, but was afraid to even think of her now. Eva was there with him, somewhere in this thick soup of minds, she knew about Shannon, and he hoped she didn't think of Shannon – didn't consider her as a Siren for them to seek out and devour to add to the Family.

At first Stanley despaired until he realized he was different from the other mental voices – the hundreds of thousands of minds all around him – there was something different about him. He did not slavishly embrace his "family." He still retained much of what made him who he was. He knew his best course of action was to be still and patient. He needed to listen to the minds around him and learn. Stanley stopped struggling against his situation and grew quiet. He sensed a certain restlessness within The Fog. He tried to determine what it was and he was frightened when he realized he could sum up the nature of the growing restlessness.

The Fog was getting hungry.

*****

The storm had passed. The sun had come out and a wave of humidity enveloped them. It seemed the temperature rose 10 degrees since they entered the police station earlier.

"This Southern humidity is one thing I won't miss once I head back to California. My God, how do you *stand* it?" he muttered as he turned up the SUV's air-conditioner.

"It gets much worse than this in the summer." Shannon said absently, as she buckled herself into her seat. "Believe it or not, you get used to it."

She lapsed back into silence as she gazed off somewhere beyond the parking lot. He knew she was looking into a place he could not see.

The humid air enveloped him like a glove. Beneath his suit, he felt sweat soaking through the armpits of his dress shirt and a wet line forming down his back. He loosened his tie and undid the top couple of buttons. He was grateful that the SUV's a/c kicked in quickly to provide some relief.

Clive didn't like Shannon's silence. She had been quiet ever since they left the interrogation room. He did not like her silence over what had happened to Stanley. She needed to talk about it – deal with it. She needed to deal with what had really happened and not the story they had pieced together for the local authorities.

He knew this from experience. He'd had no one to talk to about this and he wished he had. He had been faced with this thing for over a year now – it had stolen someone close to him and he was determined to stop it.

He watched Shannon closely for nightmares. Thus far, there had been none, except the normal reaction to a traumatic event. It interrupted her rest. Dark circles had formed beneath her brown eyes. He knew she awoke several times during the night. She would pick Chester up and cuddle him for a while. The cat seemed to be the only thing that comforted her right now.

He had not had any nightmares either, mostly because he simply hadn't been sleeping deeply enough. He grew more uneasy by the day. He knew The Fog followed a general pattern and if it continued as it had so far, it would choose another victim soon.

He had never before been this close to discovering more about it.

*****

Stanley could feel their hunger growing. It was his hunger, too. Unlike the Others, he fought it. He had learned a great deal in a short amount of time. He had learned to move unnoticed among the others, slipping in and out of conversations, absorbing information. He learned their hunger was tied to their reproductive urge. They must eat to grow their numbers – consciousness, soul – whatever it was called.

He was now part of that whole. His existence was not merely his own anymore, but he had learned how to cache pieces of himself – his humanity – without alerting the Family. For the most part, what They knew, he knew. He discovered that within The Fog, there appeared to be a hierarchy – a structure. There were the quiet, dark holes of consciousness that were the Elders. The Elders quietly drove The Fog. They kept their origins a secret from the rest of the minds within The Fog. They were ancient. He knew that, but not much else.

A sudden alertness within the Family shivered like a wave through their consciousness. The rain had stopped. They would be coming out of the cave after nightfall to seek another Siren. He felt the group's deep, abiding hunger ... the urge was becoming so strong. He tucked away his thoughts of Shannon from the rest of them.

At this point, she was not considered Siren material. She would not be sought unless she did something to draw Them. They had decided to go back West. They liked the climate there and they already have a new Siren. Someone they had considered before Eva, but Eva's call had been stronger, strong enough to pull them toward this tortuously humid climate that slowed them down.

Stanley began to formulate a plan. He wanted to say good-bye to Shannon. He felt he *must* say good-bye. He simply could not let things end the way it had between them. It was unfinished business. He had thought of a plan to see her – very briefly – one last time before the hunger was too much for him to bear.

It was risky, but he carefully laid a plan he felt would work. He made a plan to see Shannon one last time.

*****

Shannon was more tired than she realized. She was weary to her very bones. The interrogation had been tough, tougher than she realized. She thought she had dealt with what had happened with a fair amount of aplomb, but going over the details with Detective Barnes had brought it all back so vividly – the shock and horror of it.

She did not eat any lunch. They ran errands for Agent Clay and then went to her apartment so that she could do laundry and grab some more clothes than what she had, as well as some other personal items.

Tragedy was no respecter of persons. Agent Clay had mercifully gone to her apartment for her and cleaned it up after the Forensics techs were finished. She did not know how she would react coming to her apartment now.

Clay, who still had her keys, unlocked the door and opened it for her. He motioned for her to wait. Ever cautious, he checked out the apartment as she stood out on the open walkway. A warm, spring wind tossed her hair and plucked at her blouse, as it begged for her attention. *It's spring in the South ... don't you want to play?* Shannon could not feel less like playing.

The big agent reappeared and motioned her in. She entered the apartment and quickly sidestepped the spot where Stanley died just inside the door. She could not help but look at the spot. There was no trace of what had happened. She faintly smelled bleach and knew Clay had worked hard to erase both the sight and the smell of Stanley's death.

She noticed he had even cleaned the kitchen. The beer bottles and pizza box had been thrown away and the trash had been taken out.

She did not realize how tense she was until Clay cleared his throat. She jumped. He put a hand on her shoulder. "Relax, Ms. Beckman. There's nothing here now."

She knew what he really meant was that there was no man-eating fog and there were no gory bits of her dead boyfriend lying around.

She laughed a little too nervously, even to her own ears. "We have been together almost every minute for three days, Agent Clay. I think you have earned the right to call me Shannon on a regular basis."

His lips twitched in the closest thing to a smile she had ever seen him produce. "Only if you call me Clive."

She managed a stiff smile. "Deal."

He looked at her with his usual unnerving intensity. "Will you be okay if I leave you alone for a couple of hours while I do some research? I know it will take a while to finish your laundry, right?"

She looked around the apartment and took a deep breath. "I think I'll be fine. I'll keep the television on to keep the demons at bay. Silence is a hungry monster that turns your thoughts against you."

A look flitted across his face and she was certain it was something like … anguish. *What has this man been through?* She wondered.

"I know exactly what you mean," he said. After a moment, he squared his big shoulders and turned to leave. "I am just a phone call away if you change your mind and need me to come back and get you."

"I know, but I think I will be fine for two hours," she said. She had spoken the words with casual humor, but she fought an urge to call Clive back after he left. She locked the door behind him.

She went around the apartment to make sure all the windows and her patio door were locked. With that done, she turned on the television and the background voices brought a sense of normalcy and familiarity that calmed her. A small utility closet near the kitchen housed a small capacity washer and dryer. She put in a load of the clothes she had worn over the past couple of days. She took her bag into the bedroom and raided her closest to find her bigger suitcase. She chose some other outfits and went to her chest of drawers to get some more clean bras and panties. She glanced over and caught sight of her rumpled bed.

It was the one thing Clive had missed. The bed was still unmade since the night Stanley had died. She had made love with him in that bed only an hour or so before he died. She tore her eyes from the bed and bit back tears as she gathered more laundry for things she wanted to take but still needed to be laundered. She did not know how long Clive meant for her to stay in his custody, so she packed for several days.

She called her boss while the laundry ran. It was her supervisor – Carrie Maxwell. Carrie was her law firm's equivalent to what Stanley had been at Hill, Druthers, and Matheson.

"Shannon, how are you doing? I have not heard from you since that night. They are saying that it was a serial killer. Is that true?" Carrie's voice was more excited than sympathetic and Shannon didn't want to deal with her.

Shannon got right to the point. "That's what the police and the FBI are calling it. I have been put in protective custody and I just wanted to extend my vacation time, if that's okay."

"Absolutely! You have like a months' worth saved up and the bosses say that you can take as long as you need. You don't have to worry about your job. Just stay safe." There was a note of actual sincerity in Carrie's voice, which raised Shannon's opinion of her by a notch.

When she finished her call, she worked at folding and packing the clothes that had already dried and throwing the last small load in the dryer. When that was done, she found herself drawn back to the bedroom and the unmade bed. She felt so weary and soul sick. She kicked off her shoes and climbed into the bed and covered herself with the soft blankets.

She could smell Stanley's shampoo on the pillow next to her and she could smell his scent on the sheets and blankets. She cocooned herself in the bed clothes and inhaled this physical proof of her lover. Her throat tightened and she curled up into a ball.

She fell asleep with tear streaks drying on her cheeks.

*****

Shannon knew it was a dream when she found herself was standing in her favorite Thai restaurant and she could not remember how she got there. She and Stanley had eaten there so many times. Now, it was quiet and deserted. She was standing near the front of the restaurant, not far from their favorite table right in front of the establishment's large glass windows.

The restaurant was never deserted. She looked toward the windows only to find she could not see anything because a thick, gray fog was pressed against the glass like a blanket. The sight of the fog caused her to gasp and back away. The fog swirled and pressed harder against the glass – a hungry animal that wanted to get at her.

The front door opened and she backed further away, her heart pounded a powerful Samba. A male figure materialized in the fog beyond the glass door, but when he stepped into the restaurant, she recognized him.

It was Stanley. He turned and carefully closed the door to shut out the fog.

Shannon rushed to him and he caught her up in his arms. Hot tears rolled down her cheeks. She looked into and saw that his silver eyes sparkled with tears.

"Oh, baby ... I love you so much. I have missed you! It's been agony without you. How are you here?"

"I have missed you too, Shannon. I have missed you every minute," he said. He laughed as she joyfully pressed ardent kisses to his face, his hands, and his throat. He smiled and gripped her shoulders to put her gently away from him.

"We don't have much time, Sweetheart. The Others will notice I'm gone soon."

He guided her to their favorite table near the window. She eyed the window warily. Following her line of sight, he glanced toward the window and nodded solemnly in understanding.

"Don't worry about Them for now, They don't know I'm here. I want to keep it that way."

Shannon's eyes snapped back from the window to his face, then back to the fog swirling against the glass. "You can do that? What is that thing?"

"It's more like 'What are *They*,' but that is a discussion I don't have time for."

He hooked a finger under her chin to draw her eyes back to him. "I came to say good-bye. We're moving west – away from here ... away from *you*."

"You mean they won't be coming for me?" The relief she felt made her feel guilty.

"No. I have managed to keep you hidden in my thoughts – away from Them. They can't tempt you to fall if they don't notice you, and you don't have the weaknesses of a Siren ... the weaknesses that would call to Them and turn their attention to you."

She shook her head as if the physical motion would clear the confusion from it. "Weakness?"

Over Stanley's shoulder, the gray/black mass agitated – the lazy drifts and swirls became more fevered. The fog bank pressed harder against the glass – pushing against it – she could tell by the way the mass thickened and flattened.

He glanced back, nervous. He took one of her hands in his, and it seemed he was about to speak, but then something flickered within his silver eyes – there was a sudden darkening of his expression. His face went blank for a moment.

She became frightened, but he was back in a mere instant.

A small sound drew her eyes away from him. A crack had begun to stitch its way up the window as the glass was placed under greater stress. The fog now churned furiously.

He cupped her face and drew her eyes to him again. He lowered his mouth to hers and kissed her deeply. She clung to him – her tears rolled down her cheeks between them – anointing their lips.

When he pulled back, she knew he was going to leave. There was a finality to his words. "I have to go, baby. You need to wake up and you need to do it now ... I'm new at this and I can't hold them back from my thoughts much longer ..."

A myriad of fractures began to develop – she could hear the glass creak and crackle. Terror, like some drug injected directly into her veins, took her in its grip. Her heart leapt into a furious gallop.

"Wake up, Shannon," he said.

"I don't know how ...." Her voice was a fearful whisper.

"I'm sorry to do this baby, but you really need to wake THE FUCK UP!" he yelled as he drew back his hand and slapped her with a jarring force as the window glass shattered and the fog bank exploded into the restaurant. The grey/black mass came at her with the force of a flood.

Shannon screamed and put up her hands to fight back ...

*****

... Shannon fought a man who was struggling with her in her bed. He gripped her shoulders and she fought him wildly and began screaming. He quickly covered her mouth to muffle the screams.

"Sssshhhh ... Shannon, you're safe, you're safe now ... it's okay ... it's okay ..."

She slowly began to recognize her surroundings. She was in bed in her apartment. Oddly, she was on her knees, and she now recognized Agent Clay. He had apparently come in to find her in the middle of her nightmare and tried to wake her. He was also kneeling on the bed with her, holding her tightly around the waist with one hand and his other hand covered her mouth. His icy blue eyes were honed in on her with a laser focus. He removed his hand from hand from her mouth when he saw that she appeared to have come to her senses.

"Are you okay, Shannon?"

She collapsed against the big man and began to cry, and she hated herself for it. She still trembled as the terror of the nightmare still clung to her. She sobbed against his broad chest, and wrapped her arms around him as if she were lost at sea and he was the only life preserver in sight. Her tears wetted part of his white shirt and tie.

His vice-like grip on her loosened and he gently held her and stroked her hair. He lowered his head and murmured comforting nonsense against her ear.

She did not know when the moment changed for her, but she knew it was she that initiated the contact. She turned her head toward his murmuring mouth and she kissed his lips. It was the softest of contact, but she felt the gentle pressure of his lips against hers and she suddenly wanted more. She pulled back only a tiny fraction. She did not dare look into his eyes. She focused on his mouth, which she noticed for the first time, was well-shaped for sensuality.

Clive Clay went very, very still ... in an almost frightening way. Shannon was emboldened that he did not immediately pull away. The contact changed the dynamic of their situation instantly. She felt a shock of white-hot desire shoot through her and she pressed her mouth to his again. The same desire that now electrified her, sent her heart racing faster when she felt him respond.

Clive began kissing her back. At first, his return kiss was of the experimental kind. He moved his mouth softly against hers – gently stepping into unfamiliar territory. His kiss grew more insistent by degrees. She sensed he was surprised by his own reaction. His hand that had gently, and innocently, caressed her back moments before now moved down with purpose to the small of her back and he pressed her body closer against him.

His response to her began a fierce chain reaction. She moved her hands along his back – ignoring the firearm strapped against his ribs, beneath his arm, in a shoulder-holster – and caressed him sensually, exploring him. Her mouth became more insistent and Clive took over. He opened his mouth slightly and she groaned and opened hers and the kiss deepened, becoming more frantic.

Her groan appeared to create a deep response in him. She felt his tongue enter her mouth and she thought she would lose her mind.

She wanted him.

She slid her hands down to his hips and pulled him closer and he brought one hand up to cradle the back of her head. His large hand pulled her head back to give him access to her throat. He lowered his head and began to kiss and taste the length of her throat and the curves and hollows where her neck met her shoulder. He tugged the collar of her blouse aside to do so. He worked his way back up to her mouth she brought her hands up to touch his face and she ran her fingers through his dark hair. She inhaled his groan against her mouth. The urgency of the moment grew.

Clive pulled back from her abruptly. His shocked expression told her it was over and worked the same as a splash of cold water.

"What the hell are we doing?" he asked as he disentangled himself from her.

He backed from his kneeling position on the bed, stood up, and moved away. She could not help but notice he was aroused before he turned away from her.

She was confused and a little ashamed, but not as much as she probably should have been. She knew she would have to think on this later and sort out the "whys" of what had just happened and why she had started it.

"Clive ... I'm ... I'm sorry ... I don't know why I did that ... I ..." her voice trailed off. She needed him to understand. She hated the sound of tears in her voice. She had just experienced extreme terror followed shortly by extreme passion and now she felt drained, unsure, and confused.

He ran his hands through his hair to straighten what she had mussed. He kept his back to her, but she could see from the set of his shoulders that he regained his self-control by the evolution of his shoulders from relaxed to straight. She moved to the edge of her bed and sat there with her feet on the floor. She waited.

Finally, he turned around. His icy gaze gave nothing away, but he did not seem angry. "You need to finish packing. I'll wait for you in the living room," he said quietly as he turned to leave the bedroom.

"What about what just happened? Are you angry?" She knew she was pushing her luck, but she had to ask. She hated that she felt like she was on the brink of tears again, like some little girl.

He stopped and turned to look back at her. Something flickered in his eyes, but it was too brief for her to recognize. He seemed tense, but her question caused him to take a deep breath. His shoulders sagged wearily. He put his hands in his pants pockets.

He appeared to choose his words carefully. "What just happened was unprofessional and *wildly* inappropriate – particularly on my part, but I don't think we need to talk about it right now. Let's just chalk it up to a reaction to heightened emotions. We'll discuss what led up to it when we get back to the motel."

Shannon nodded, mutely. Clive left the bedroom and she slowly went about the completion of her packing.

Her last chore was to finally make her bed. She changed the sheets and took more care than usual to make sure every wrinkle was tugged out.

She took a look around the room before she turned her back and allowed Clive to help her with her bags. She had a feeling she would not see this apartment again for a long time.

*****

Back at the motel, Clive hated to leave Shannon again, but he could not be near her for a while. He had already been on his evening run, so he headed to the motel's tiny "work-out room" to pump some iron. The tiny room had a large Pilate's ball, a treadmill, an exercise bike that had seen better days, but there was a weight bench and some free weights.

As he worked out, he went back over what had happened with Shannon earlier. His own reaction to her startled him. He felt guilty. Ashley had been dead for almost a year, but he had not been with anyone else since her. He had been too busy trying to stop the thing that killed her. Even if he could get past the guilt – the feelings of being unfaithful – Shannon was under his watch. It was unprofessional. This was not like him.

He knew he would not let it happen again, but in order to do that he had to understand how he had let it almost get out of control. He had come very close to taking her right there on the bed she had shared with Stanley. It was not just heat of the moment ... it was an urge that was so powerful ... it almost felt like something he *needed* to do ... *had* to do.

He pumped the maximum he could bench press without a spotter and tried not to think about how sweet her mouth tasted or how good her body felt against him. He just knew he could not allow himself to be distracted.

By the time he completed his workout, Clive felt ready to talk to Shannon about her dream.

*****

Shannon sat on the bed and stroked Chester. It helped soothe her nerves. Clive's odd combination of intensity and indecipherable moods and expression, made him intimidating at times. She heard him outside the motel room door as he swiped his key card. She noticed his laser-beam intensity had come down a notch or two since they had left her apartment, but judging by the sweat soaked workout clothes, she saw the price he paid for his newfound sense of calm.

"Are you hungry for supper, yet? I know you didn't eat your lunch." Clive said as he tossed his key card on the table by her bed.

Shannon was surprised to realize she was actually famished, but didn't want to go out. "Can we do take out, though?

Clive nodded absently. "Chinese?"

She nodded and stroked Chester. Chester looked up at Clive. "*Meow*."

Shannon looked up at Clive earnestly. "I agree with Chester. Bring beer."

Clive froze for a moment … then, his lips twitched and he nodded. "Give me a few minutes to shower and I'll go grab the food. I saw a menu in the drawer over there. Pick out what you want."

Later, as they sat at the table, eating, Clive finally addressed the dream.

"So … can you tell me about the dream?"

Shannon noted his careful phrasing as he avoided any mention of him coming into her bedroom or what had happened afterward.

"It wasn't an erotic dream," she said. He looked relieved.

She told him about the restaurant, Stanley, and about the fog at the windows.

"He said for me not to worry – that the fog bank was going to be heading 'west' – whatever that means. He also said that 'They' (she used air-quotes) would not be coming for me because I did not have the normal 'weaknesses of a Siren.' He indicated that those weaknesses are what actually draws the monster man-eating fog."

"Weaknesses? What does that mean?" Clive's dark brows furrowed. "I have been following this thing for almost two years. I've never been this close. I have tried to connect the victims in all kinds of ways. I can connect most of them through just familiarity – obvious connection such as with Stanley and Eva, but there were others that I never could figure out."

Shannon pondered. "It seems to me there is an element of both things that normally draws the fog ... this 'weakness' that Stanley mentioned, but I also think familiarity is involved, too."

Clive laced his fingers behind his head and leaned back. He closed his eyes for a moment. "I could not locate the element of familiarity for at least two of the victims such as the last two victims before Eva. I couldn't connect them to each other -- they were all in Oklahoma, and she lived here in Tennessee."

She shrugged and took a pull from her beer. "Then, you've missed something. Something that is going to be harder to find ... maybe you just need another perspective. I am happy to help. God knows I have nothing else to do right now. Besides, since Stanley indicated the fog would not come after me, I'm surprised you have kept me in protective custody."

"It's temporary ... just until I can see that the fog has moved on, then you can get back to your normal life."

"My life will never be normal again, Clive. *Never*," she blinked back tears and took another swig of beer.

They were both quiet for a long time. Finally, Shannon changed the subject, going back to what Stanley had said. "For what it's worth, I have had time to think about this and I believe the weaknesses Stanley spoke of are like ... weaknesses of character."

Clive's eyes suddenly pinned her to her seat. "What do you mean?"

She squirmed. "Well, I like to think I'm a pretty good judge of character and Stanley was really a good guy. His cheating with Eva was unusual for him and I think he felt really guilty – over-the-top guilty. His giving in to temptation was a weakness of character – albeit a temporary one. The guilt was a negative emotion – maybe that is a factor. I don't know, but I think the cheating is what drew Its attention to Stanley. And ... Eva ... I remember a long time ago that Stanley had mentioned that she was kind of needy ... lonely. She had a major lack of self-confidence. It kept her in a nowhere relationship with that idiot, Bart, until he dumped her for some health club chick."

Clive's guard dropped and she could read his expression. She could tell that this was something he thought might actually be helpful.

"Yes, what you said correlates to what I learned about her during investigation. Her mother said she and her daughter were very close," he said, absently. She could tell he was processing the information. Suddenly, his expression changed to alarm "Wait ... this afternoon ... you and me ... would that have brought its attention to you?"

She shook her head. "I honestly don't know, but I don't think a simple kiss would do it."

He favored her with a smile. Her heart skipped. It was the first time she had ever seen him really smile. She discovered Clive Clay was a real lady-killer when he smiled. "I didn't think there was anything 'simple' about that kiss ... and ... it almost turned into something else."

Shannon fought the urge to smile back. It was difficult – far more difficult than she would have thought. She quietly asked, "Why did you stop?"

He looked away from her. He had let his guard down enough for her to read him. She accepted that as the compliment it was. He trusted her. His expression was a complex mix of fond recollection, pain, and grief. He took a pull from his own beer.

"I felt guilty," he finally answered.

She waited.

He took a deep breath. "I was married for about four years. Her name was Ashley ... she died about a year ago. It was the fog bank that killed her. It killed her right in front of me. Anyway, earlier ... in your bedroom ... that was the first time in several years I had been that close to anyone other than Ashley. It felt like cheating ... I just couldn't do it. I do find you attractive and I wanted to take you right there ... but my own good sense kicked back in. I know that in time, the 'cheating' feeling will go away, but that's not the only reason I stopped. I am better than that. I am an FBI agent and you are a vulnerable woman in my custody. Ethically ... it is out of the question."

So many questions ran through her mind, but she asked the one that surfaced first. "What was Ashley's weakness, Clive? There had to be one for The Fog to come after her."

He was quiet for so long that she did not think he would answer the question.

He tipped his beer bottle and emptied it before he finally spoke. "I was not the initial agent assigned to investigate the disappearances. They had been going on for a few months. There had been some in southern California around the eastern side of the state. We lived in San Bernardino – that is the field office I work out of -- and there was a disappearance near there, so I was initially called in to consult. Normally, I work criminal investigations ... I don't do this X-Files shit."

After bitter laugh, he continued, "I started really digging in. The agents assigned to the case only had the smallest of leads and frankly, their minds were not open enough to look at the facts. I said I don't do X-Files, but I'm open-minded. I'm a pragmatist that way. So, I started finding some weird connections between a lot of the victims and I think I was paying more attention to what the people were saying about the victims.

"You know the story ... there were 'bad dreams' and 'sleep walking' and the victims' appearance was enhanced or changed right before they disappeared," he paused to open another beer.

"It turns out that the nearest disappearance in our area was a personal training instructor from a local health club, one of which my wife was a member. The guy's name was Colby Hannon," he continued. "Ashley's reaction to his disappearance – and it was all over the local news – was really far more than it should have been ... or rather ... there was a quality to her grief that was more than what I thought it should be."

Shannon watched him closely. "I would imagine that you're a hard man to hide things from, especially if it's someone you are very close to."

He had been alternately contemplating the table and his beer bottle, which he rolled gently between his hands, but his gaze moved to her face. He gave her a rueful smile, "You would be correct. It's a curse for anyone who gets close to me."

He moved his gaze back to the bottle and he slowly rolled it between his palms, as if the action would conjure the past, so that he could accurately recall every detail.

"Ashley started sleep walking ..." he said, quietly.

She felt like crying. "Oh, no ... Clive ... I'm so sorry ..."

"Yeah, me too," he said. It appeared to be physically painful for him to relate the story. He stretched his neck from one side to the other. "After all I already knew, and with her being connected to the victim through the health club, I knew she must have been involved with Hannon."

There was a long silence. Finally, he sighed. "I can't blame her entirely. I was not unhappy in our marriage, but I had two wives ... Ashley and my work – at least that's what she used to say whenever we argued about it. So, I was never lonely. I was in love with my wife, and I loved my work, so I was happy in both places. Ashley didn't have that ... she liked her work as a preschool teacher, but it wasn't her passion. She loved me, but after four years of not having me around for long, long hours ... I know she had to have been very lonely at times."

She wanted to reach out to him, but she didn't dare. She did not think he would accept comfort in regards to this matter at the moment.

"I was working late the first night she had the dreams. She told me the next day that she ended up in the kitchen – splayed out naked on the table. She tried to laugh it off, but I could tell it scared her. She made some vague mention of seeing a fog bank in our yard. I knew she was leaving out details because she was worried that I would think she was crazy.

"The second night, she ended up on the bedroom floor – naked – but she had bruises on her. She was pretty shaken up by that one and begged me to be home early. I did and we went to bed at the same time. I fell asleep and woke up because she was gone. I jumped out of bed, and grabbed my firearm. Thankfully, our home sits on a couple of acres, so it's pretty well hidden from our neighbors. I was naked. If the neighbors were close, they would have gotten an eye full."

He returned to his careful rolling of the beer bottle. "She was laying on her back in the driveway by the car. Her legs spread wide open – bent at the knees. There was a fog drifting around *everything*. It was hard to explain what I saw ... it was a lot like you described with what you saw the night the thing came to Stanley in your bedroom ... it looked like she was being fucked silly by a shadow man formed from the fog ... her eyes were half closed. There was a full moon that lit up everything like it was daylight and I could see that her eyes were rolled back so far that the whites were showing. She was screaming in pleasure at first ... but then ... then things started to change.

"The shadow man sort of dissolved and the fog tentacles began to wrap themselves around her arms and legs ... one large one was already up inside her and then it started funneling into her eyes, her mouth, her ears ... her screams of pleasure turned to screams of pain like I've never heard ..."

Clive's face was anything but impassive now. His eyes glistened with unshed tears of rage, pain, and grief. Shannon could not help but reach out to gently touch one of his hands, temporarily halting the roll of the beer bottle.

"What did you do?" she asked.

"You have to understand that all of this happened in a manner of seconds," he said. She was encouraged that he did not move away the hand she gently held. He let go of the bottle and wiped at his eyes with his other hand. "At first, I was so shocked, I didn't know what was happening ... my eyes couldn't decipher what I was seeing ... but, her screams shook me out of the shock. I dropped into a shooter's stance and began firing at the fog around her. It passed right through, of course and hit her car. I ran toward her and even got hold of one of her arms ... by then her screams and turned to these fucking ... awful, wet, gagging sounds ... and she ... like the shadow man ... was being almost instantaneously dissolved."

Tears were rolling down her face. She was more grateful than ever that Clive had covered her eyes when Stanley was killed in her apartment. She was fairly certain her mind would have snapped if she had witnessed the whole thing.

"I touched ... It ... the fog. It actually has some substance and it didn't like me trying to take its meal ... It ... bit me on the wrist but I didn't let go ... another tentacle came out of the fog and wrapped around my waist. It picked me up and threw me about six feet. It would have been farther, but a tree stopped me. Hitting the tree knocked the wind out of me, but I rolled and got back on my feet, but by then ... there was nothing left ... nothing ... she had been naked, so there were no clothes left behind ... just her wedding ring." His voice had narrowed to a whisper. He tugged his hand free of her soft touch and covered his face and broke down.

She did not know him well enough to wrap her arms around him, but she wanted to do just that – anything to comfort him. His story brought back her own recent ordeal and she cried, too.

Clive had rolled up his sleeves and taken off his tie when they had settled down to eat. She looked at his left wrist and noticed – for the first time – a rectangular-ish scar, about the size of a common adhesive bandage. It was puckered, with pinkish edges and white in the center. It obviously a newer scar.

She could not help but wonder -- *How in the hell do we stop something like this?*

*****

Cheveyo sat on the floor of his grandfather's pueblo home. Evening had brought the colder temperatures and he always enjoyed speaking with his grandfather by the fire pit. Elaborate rugs, made by his grandmother, served as a mat.

Currently, his grandfather looked deep in thought as he considered everything Cheveyo had told him about what he had found at the crater.

They spoke in low voices, respectful of the gravity of what had happened and what must be done. His father was a traditionalist and continued to observe the old ways.

"I am too old now, Cheveyo, son of my son. We knew almost from your birth that you would be a Shadow Warrior and you were named for this," he said. "Now, you must gather the others ... Hototo, Pachu'a, Wikvaya, and Qaletaga. I will speak with the other elders.

"We were always the peaceful ones, but the desert demon is old and we are the oldest of those who walked this land and it has always been our responsibility to watch for the danger, but all of the native tribes are in danger from this demon. You will need to reach out to as many tribes as possible. We will need help. This is a large undertaking," he said. He stirred the fire with a handmade poker.

Cheveyo nodded. "I will do what is needed."

Cheveyo did not need to know when to begin. His dreams had already told him that the time would be very near when his path is crossed by the white man and woman who have set out to chase the demon.

He would lay plans and wait until he met those who were unknowingly destined to help him.

*****

Clive found Shannon to be extremely stubborn, but fortunately her actual helpfulness outweighed the former. She insisted on helping him search through material on Eva Shelby to find a connection between her and the three victims in Oklahoma. She had brought her laptop from home and asked him constant questions.

He understood that she needed to "do something" to help. He also understood there were a tangle of reasons for this and he could guess at some of them: the need for distraction from her grief; the desire to feel like she had a hand in stopping the force that took her lover from her; and finally the simplest of reasons – cabin fever.

He not only understood her unspoken reasons, he shared them. Besides, after the kiss they shared the day before, and his emotional confession that night, they needed to do something productive.

So, they embarked on a day of research. Clive revisited a lot of the data he had on the three Slocum, Oklahoma victims prior to Eva.

"I can see the connection between the last two victims before Eva – they were dating each other -- Linda Merrill and Bill Bullard," he said, as he tossed his pen onto the table and rubbed his hands over his face. They had been researching these people's lives for nearly three hours. "But, I still cannot connect the first one in Oklahoma – Carlos Vega – with the other two."

"I think I know what the connection is …" Shannon said, absently. She had her honey-colored hair up in a ponytail and she had forgone makeup. She looked like a high school girl.

She motioned for him to come around to look at her laptop screen with her. He brought his chair around and sat close. He noticed her hair smelled like a very pleasant herbal shampoo.

He noticed she had the social networking site – Facebook – open on her laptop. She had three tabs open on her computer.

She looked excited.

"I hate to break this to you, but one of the many things we checked out was their 'friends' on social media sites and none of these people, except for the two who were dating, were friends on Facebook," he said.

She grinned. "I know that, but they are all 'online' types. They all have profiles and I have been studying information. Carlos, Bill, and Linda all like a lot of the same movies – horror flicks, mostly, but they also all have a thing for vampire fiction. So did Eva. Stanley told me her bookshelves were lined with every conceivable popular title."

He nodded. "That's true."

"I got to thinking that if they were such over-the-top big fans of vampire fiction, then maybe they would be involved in some of those online chat rooms and fan fiction sites," she suggested.

Clive was hopeful, but did not want to get excited just yet. "Yes, but if they were on those sites, wouldn't they want to be friends on social media, too?"

She shook her head, ponytail bouncing merrily. "Not necessarily. A lot of the profiles for these groups are anonymous. People are paranoid these days – and rightly so. They don't use their real names because this is part of their lonely fantasy. I bet if you check Eva's online activity more closely, you will find that she was part of a vampire chat group.

Clive jumped up and pulled out a file in a nearby box. "You know what? I think I remember seeing something in the stuff they pulled from her laptop and internet files."

He studied the file for a few moments and he finally allowed himself to become optimistic. His instincts told him Shannon was onto something. "Eva was only on one chat room regularly. It was a book discussion group called Tomes of Blood."

Shannon looked positively electrified. "I knew it! I will bet if you check the activity of the others, at least one of them was on that site, too."

Clive made a call to the Oklahoma detective working the case. He was on the phone for a while. When he got off he could not stop himself from smiling at Shannon as she sat there – her brown eyes wide with excitement.

"He confirmed they were all part of the Tomes of Blood book discussion chat room. We also confirmed that the management at Carlos' workplace stated they were investigating him for embezzlement and friends admitted he had a fling with Linda that Bill did not know about. To recap, Carlos is connected to Linda the second victim, who is obviously connected to Bill ... who I think we can assume was connected to Eva somehow ... ... so, it seems your theory about character weaknesses is valid in determining potential victims."

"Sirens," Shannon corrected, softly.

"Sirens," he amended.

She leaned back with her hands laced behind her head. He averted his eyes immediately when he found them drawn to her breasts which were displayed so prettily in that position.

Her eyes were far away as she formed a thought. He waited in an expectant silence.

"It seems to me that the internet chat room connection would not be enough. I will bet that if you check out Eva's records, you're going to find some kind of motel bill or something ..."

"We thought of that and there was nothing ..." he said. "She did call in sick for two days earlier that week, but there was no usage on her credit card. She took out some money the weekend before, though."

"Hmm ...." She chewed her bottom lip. "What about Bill?"

He pulled out the records and studied. He found something. "He rented a motel room the same day Eva first called in sick. Stayed all night ... but it was in Little Rock, Arkansas." He quickly pulled out an atlas. After consulting the map, he slapped the table. "That is just about exactly halfway between Slocum, Oklahoma and Nashville, Tennessee."

"She took out *cash*, Clive," she noted, with a raised eyebrow. "Did she take out a larger amount than what would be normal for her? She lives in Nashville. Her mortgage was kind of high, she had a car payment and school loans from her paralegal training ...the woman was on a budget. She had also broken up with her boyfriend of what ...five years? She met Bill out there. I would bet Chester's next meal that she is smarter than anyone gave her credit for ... she has a conservative mother from whom she would have hidden a tryst ... she was lonely ... and Bill was someone who had mutual interests. Check the motel Little Rock. I think you'll find out that she was there."

Clive got on the phone with the local authorities. By the time he was off the phone, he felt something shimmering within his heart that he had not known in a long time. He smiled at Shannon. "Yep, you get Chester's next meal. Someone said a woman fitting Eva's description with Tennessee plates came and met him in the motel lounge and stayed the night with him."

His hope was dampened a bit when he received a call back from the Oklahoma police. The voice at the other end was a gruff, Okie accent. "Agent Clay?"

Clive's instincts told him this would be bad news. He braced himself. "Yes, is this Chief Jay?"

A grim chuckle at the other end of the connection answered before the Chief said a word. "It sure is. I'm afraid I have some news – there has been another disappearance. I thought I would phone you since you have already been working the case."

"I appreciate the courtesy, Chief. What information do you have about the victim?"

The sound of a papers shuffling and a keyboard clicking evoked memories of the Chief's office. "It was a white male ... in his 30's. His name was Chad Moore. He worked at the hospital with Linda Merrill, the second victim. His family called the police this morning when he didn't come down to breakfast. Apparently, he lives with his sister and her family. Anyway, when officers arrived, they found the same mess as with the other three – only in Moore's bed. He apparently sleeps in his underwear. There was just the mess of drying bodily waste in the bed and a pair of underwear. There was also a tiny piece of what the coroner believes to be muscle tissue."

Some expression on his face, alarmed Shannon because she had stopped working on her laptop and now watched him closely. She was very still and very pale.

"I have been investigating the two disappearances here in Nashville. I will be heading back your way as soon as possible."

"Good," the chief sounded relieved. "We need the help."

Clive ended the call and tossed his cell phone on the table by his own laptop.

"There's been another victim, hasn't there?" Shannon's expression caused him some concern. Her brown eyes intense and dark in her pale face.

He told her the details and said, "It looks like Stanley managed to keep it away from you. It's moved on. You should be relieved."

"That thing killed Stanley ... I won't be 'relieved' until it's destroyed," she said. There was steel beneath her words that Clive would not have expected.

He got up and closed his laptop. He picked up his file box and began tossing files inside.

"What are you doing?" she asked, but her tone told him she already suspected what he was doing.

"I'm packing up. I've got to leave for Oklahoma as soon as possible before the trail gets cold. It's time you went home. I think you're safe now," he said. He quickly completed packing his files. In just three short days, he had grown used to having Shannon around. Today, she had practically become his partner with her valuable insight and hard work researching.

His mind was racing ahead to what he would need to do when he reached Oklahoma. He moved to pack up his clothes. He stopped suddenly – in the process of folding and shoving clothes into a large duffel on his bed -- when he realized Shannon had been silent as a stone. She had not moved from her seat. He looked over at her and found she watched him with a dark look.

Her expression was mutinous. Her tone would brook no refusal. "I'm going with you."

"No," he said. "You're not trained and it's too dangerous."

She did not answer him. She got up and began to pack her own belongings. "If you don't take me with you, then I'll just go it alone. If something happens to me, then at least you had the chance to take me with you."

He could tell she meant it. He knew he shouldn't bring her, but some part of him knew he needed her. He also knew he shouldn't use her this way, her ideas and the fact that The Fog might still be drawn to her, could make this a deadly venture. Still, he could not allow her to go running out there on her own.

He steeled himself against his waffling emotions and made a decision he hoped he would not regret later.

He decided to take Shannon with him to Oklahoma.

*****

The trip to Oklahoma was long and uneventful, but not boring. Shannon used Clive as her sounding board for her theories about The Fog. For some reason, his silence on the drive had a "dark" feeling to it and it made her nervous, which made her talk more than usual.

Adding to her chatter, Chester apparently did not like to travel. In between his yowling in his pet carrier, he would either nap or throw up. They had to make more frequent stops to drug the nervous cat.

They got their food from fast food chains off I-40 and kept on driving. Chester finally calmed down when she pulled him from his carrier and held him as they drove. She had him swaddled like a human baby and he seemed to like it. At least he shut up and went to sleep – which was close enough to "like" for her. However, his proximity to Clive made the agent break into bouts of sneezing. They had to pull over to dig out his allergy medicine.

She brought a notebook and made notes along the way. She recorded her own thoughts and Clive's short answers to her many questions. She analyzed the data and an idea began to occur to her. More like a strategy. The very idea made her stomach clench, and she shelved it until they finally reached Slocum, Oklahoma, where they settled into a motel. Clive refused to let her come with him to see the police chief.

"It's not professional How the hell would I explain the laundry list I have brought with me? Let's see ... I have brought the cat from the first Tennessee victim ... oh, and I have also brought the girlfriend of the last Tennessee victim who is also in my custody. Yeah ... this is not an ideal situation, Shannon," he said.

She waited at the motel, but she could not stop pacing. The idea that the fog had killed yet another person, and they couldn't seem to stop it, tore at her heart and mind. She thought she knew a way to stop it from killing other people, at least for a while. She was just afraid of what Clive would think of her idea.

She suspected Clive's frustration outweighed her own by a metric ton. He had been dealing with this entity and its path of destruction for far longer than she. Each death seemed to add another weight on his soul. She could tell this time was no different by the look on his face when he returned.

He sat down in the chair – so similar to all the other motel room chairs she had ever seen – put his elbows on the table and his face in his hands. He was comfortable enough around her now that he let his guard down and his emotions show. She took it for the compliment it was. He sighed and rubbed his face. He looked haggard and older.

"It was bad," he said. "The Fog left behind a couple of small chunks of muscle tissue. It was hungry, I guess because there was no report of bad dreams beforehand ... It didn't have much time to 'romance' him, probably because of us. Stanley managed to keep it off of you."

Her whole body was suddenly a lead weight sinking in a bottomless sea. She sat down heavily in the chair on the opposite side of the table.

"If that weren't bad enough," he continued, "it seems he recently had his heart broken by his girlfriend, who stepped out on him when she found out about his little fling with Linda."

"Oh ... god .... She will probably be next!" She put her hands to her mouth and desperate tears filled her eyes. "We've got to stop this thing, Clive. I have an idea ... I wasn't sure if we should try it, but now I think it might work."

He sat up straighter and trained his laser gaze on her. "What's your idea?"

She steeled herself against his reaction. "I think we need to have sex."

*****

Clive could not believe his ears. "Wait? *What*?"

Shannon's sincerity showed in her solemn expression. It was as if she had delivered the news of a loved one's death.

"We need to have sex," she repeated.

"Sex?"

"Yes. Sex."

"You and me?"

"Yes."

He sat back in his chair. He was stunned. "I'm sorry, Shannon, but you're going to have to lay out the logic behind that statement because I cannot for the life of me fathom how you think that would help or help stop The Fog in any way."

She blushed a bright shade of red, but she pushed forward. She sat up straighter in her seat and looked at him with complete sincerity. She folded her hands on the table almost primly. "Well, it seems to me that The Fog had a taste of me when it got Stanley. It's attracted to negative feelings like guilt, regret, lust ... and, based on that kiss a couple of days ago, I think it's obvious that we're attracted to each other, but you've got guilt over your wife and I'm missing Stanley and we've got a thing called decorum that tempers our instincts. We have control of ourselves and don't let lust just run amok."

He listened. He was interested in where this was going. She was being quite scientific about it – it was almost amusing.

"I think we can keep anyone else from getting killed right now if we give in to that lust. We can make a loud enough 'siren call,' so to speak, to draw it back to me if we simply do what we know will make us both feel guilty – and that is give in to our lust ... our natural urges."

"Uh-huh," he grunted, in response. He leaned forward, pinning her to her seat with his gaze. He was no fool, he knew precisely how intimidating he could be. He felt a complex stir of emotions at her outrageous proposal. He was suddenly, and powerfully, pissed off and he did not want to examine why.

"There's one flaw in your plan," he said, softly.

Her wary expression told him she knew his soft tone was dangerous. "What's the flaw?"

"How do we keep that thing from killing us if we manage to attract its attention?" He rose from his chair. He felt crazy and he knew it was out of proportion to the situation. He was in front of her in an instant. He grasped her by her upper arms and yanked her to her feet. He towered over her. He wanted to shake her, but he managed to keep his temper in check "We don't know how to *kill* it! No one in two years has figured out how to defeat it, Shannon. You lost Stanley ... I lost Ashley ... I can't watch anyone else die! Do you *understand* that? Are you living in reality? *Seriously*? That is the most insane proposal I have ever fucking heard? Are you suicidal?"

It only made him angrier to see her eyes fill up with tears, which spilled over and rolled down her cheeks like liquid diamonds – the value of her big heart.

"Once it comes for me ... I plan to get information from Stanley on how to kill it," she cried. Her voice was not much more than a hoarse whisper. "I plan to look for clues how to kill it before it kills me, but I'm willing to die trying."

Her brown eyes were fathomless but determined. He felt a familiar clench low in his belly and he knew there was another part of his anatomy that would like to make decisions for him, but he had learned to ignore those impulses a long time ago. However, this time, his own toxic mix of pain, frustration, anger, grief, and guilt dulled his impulses. *What are you holding back for?* His body asked him.

Shannon's tears rolled down her face and a single tear reached the top of her delectable-looking mouth and he came undone. He let go of her upper arms and took her face in his hands and lowered his mouth to hers for a long, hard kiss. It was rough and unromantic, but it was emotionally-charged and served to spark a reaction.

She seemed surprised at first. She brought her hands to hold onto his wrists, as if she could stop him. He soon found his angry kiss became more passionate than angry. It had been a long time. He had denied himself pleasure for so long that it came back to haunt him. He reveled in the feel of the softness of her mouth against his. He pressed his thumb to her chin to encourage her mouth to open to him. Her mouth opened and a small moan escaped on a sigh into his mouth. He deepened the kiss as he began to explore the moist, velvety surfaces inside with his tongue.

After her initial shock, she began to return his kiss in kind. Her tongue slipped into his mouth and he felt her softly explore him and found it to be exciting beyond reason. He slipped his hands into her hair, enjoying the soft, silky strands between his fingers, but his hands were restless and anxious to explore this new territory.

His hands slid down her back with soft caresses against her tee-shirt and moving down her jeans to finally grip her firm, round bottom and he pulled her hard against him. She whimpered softly in arousal and he was on the verge of completely losing control when his mind finally stepped back in to take over his traitorous body.

Suddenly, he let go of her and stepped back. "I can't do this, Shannon. Not like this. This is just giving in to instincts ... It isn't the result of a decision. I need time to think and it seems I can't do that in the same room with you. I'll be back."

He took one long last look at her. He wondered if she knew how lovely and desirable she looked – her lips swollen from his kisses and her hair mussed by his hands. He wanted to rip her clothes off and mindlessly screw her until he had nothing left to give. This was the very reason he knew he had to leave.

Now.

He grabbed his keys and cell phone off the table and left her standing there looking shaken and confused.

*****

Shannon was not sure what had just happened. Clive had started this and then stopped again just as things were really getting interesting. If she were honest with herself, she would admit that she needed Clive in a very primitive-celebrate-being-alive kind of way, but her heart belonged to Stanley. It had not been but a few days since he was killed, and guilt pounded her heart like a hammer on an anvil.

How can I be attracted to someone so soon? She wondered, but already suspected it was merely lust and a need to reaffirm life. She also thought it might have something to do with the shared trauma that bonded them together.

Either way, she knew her plan would work if he would just give it a chance before anymore outsiders were killed to feed the monster. She was depressed, believing he would never go along with what she proposed. She sat down on the bed and felt foolish.

Chester jumped up and raised up on his hind legs and put his paws on either side of her neck. She looked into his eerie golden gaze and he leaned forward and nuzzled her chin. She tipped her head down and he nuzzled her cheek, her tears wetting his fur.

"*Meow,*" he said.

She smiled through her tears. "Thanks, Chester. You are an amazing kitty."

"*Meow.*" Apparently, he agreed.

After some time had passed she dried her tears of humiliation and tried to work out how she was going to face him again. She was in the middle of working out a plan to attract the monster without Clive's help when he came back.

He came in carrying a brown bag. She watched him as he wordlessly pulled out a bottle of the Glenlivet and sat it on the table. He unwrapped a couple of plastic cups that bore the motel logo. He left with the complimentary ice bucket and returned with ice. He dropped some ice in each cup and poured out about three fingers in each. He shrugged out of his jacket and tossed it on the back of a chair.

He removed his shoulder-holster rig and weapon and laid it on the table. He untucked his shirt and unbuttoned it before he turned around. His shirt now hung open to reveal a wife-beater style white tee-shirt beneath. He lifted one of the cups and handed it to her. She took it with a nod to the bottle on the table.

"You sprang for the expensive stuff. What's the occasion?"

He turned and lifted his cup and swallowed his own drink in a couple of gulps. He took a moment to enjoy the fire before he looked at her. He removed his dress shirt. Again, she noticed the wide scar that slashed around the back of his left wrist – a souvenir from The Fog. He had a Celtic cross tattooed on his right bicep. His icy-eyes were turned up to high intensity.

"It's not every day that I make a decision that is not only unprofessional, but could cost me either my job, my life, your life, or all of the above ... but ..." he paused to pour himself another drink, "that is exactly what I have done. My brain is screaming this is stupid and dangerous, my heart is screaming that I'm cheating on Ashley ... but my instincts tell me that you may be on to something ... so ... the whiskey is the only way I can shut up my head and my heart and let instinct take control." With that said, he lifted his cup to her in a salute and drained it.

Her heart sped up alarmingly. Her mouth went dry. It was her idea, but the thought of actually going to bed with Clive Clay sort of terrified her. She tore her eyes away from his and took a couple of sips of from her own cup. It took her breath away. Her hand was trembling a little. She glanced back at Clive and blushed when she saw how closely he watched her.

"Oh ... now ... Shannon ... don't tell me that you're suddenly *shy*. You don't get to be shy *now*." His voice was soft and perilously seductive. She shivered. She had never had cause to truly see this side of him before.

"I ... I am a more 'heat of the moment' kind of girl. I really don't know how to begin this. It ... it seems so c-cold and planned," she stammered. She felt ridiculous after having made this proposal to begin with. She had thought of everything except how she would actually make love with Agent Clay – the process ... the reality of it.

"I see," he said, with a lopsided grin that nearly took her breath away as efficiently as the whiskey. "Then, I suggest you drink up and we figure out how to create some 'heat of the moment.'"

She realized the Scotch whiskey was a good idea. He had a point. She normally didn't drink liquor. It wasn't her style. It seemed more formal, frequent drinkers drank whiskey. She was a casual beer and wine type.

She pushed Chester toward the edge of her bed. He took the hint, leapt down, and made himself scarce. She took a few more sips. She had only consumed about three-fourths of what he had poured, and she was already feeling it thread its way through her veins.

He untucked and removed his tee-shirt. "I have an idea," he said as he poured himself a third drink. She had never seen him shirtless before. She knew he had a tattoo on his right bicep because she had seen a little of it when he wore his short-sleeved tee-shirts to bed and for running. The full tattoo was revealed to her moments ago, but now as he turned to pour another drink, she saw that he had a fire-breathing dragon tattooed on his back. He turned back around. "Do you like music?"

"Who doesn't?" She could barely get the words out as she looked at him. His body was well-muscled. His stomach was flat and his chest was broad and lightly furred with dark hair. With his dark hair and ice-blue eyes, he looked like some dark lord standing there studying her at his leisure.

He grabbed his cell phone and located a playlist. He turned it on and sat it down on the table. The Black Crows began to play "Hard to Handle." He walked over to her and held out his hand. "Dance with me."

She put her drink on the nightstand and tried to hide her trembling when she took his hand. He pulled her to her feet and used her hand to spin her slowly as he sang with the song, "'Cause Mama I am sure hard to handle now ...'"

She laughed and it loosened the knot in her chest. "I'll bet you're hard to handle."

"Sweetheart, you have *no* idea," he said as he spun her again and then pulled her close to him, "but it looks like you're about to find out."

She slid one arm around his waist and caressed his back. His warm skin was a jolt to her libido, but she was still hesitant.

"Shut your brain and your heart *off*, Shannon," he murmured. His face was so close that his whiskey-perfumed breath stirred her hair. "Put your tray in the upright position as we are about to take off. Just let your instincts take over. We are about to be *bad*, remember?"

She closed her eyes and took a deep breath and let the whiskey in her blood help her let go. She brought her face to his chest and inhaled his scent. She pressed her lips to his skin in a series of soft, slow kisses. She reveled in the feel of his masculine skin beneath her soft lips.

His hands slid around her waist and roamed her back and then slid down again to grip her buttocks. He pulled her closer against him. She could feel his hard length against her abdomen. He was aroused. She let her hands come around to his front and she let her fingers trail paths through his chest hair and down his stomach. He was like rock encased in flesh.

A new song began, Robin Trower's "In this Place," set a sensual tone. His hands grasped the bottom of her tee-shirt and he pulled it upward until she raised her arms to allow him to pull it off over her head and toss it to the floor. She wore a simple white cotton bra. She had not thought she would need anything sexy. She looked up at his expression and saw that his eyes feasted on her generous cleavage. She was large-breasted, but not overly so.

Clive's big hands moved to the sides of her breasts and then he moved his palms to the front and let his fingers trail across the tops of the silky, twin mounds. His touch made her catch her breath.

"You are so lovely," he whispered as he lowered his head to kiss her.

The kiss was immediately passionate. His lips worked wonders as he plundered the sweet depths of her mouth with his tongue. She could not stop a small sound of hungry pleasure and she greedily and possessively began to touch him – his shoulders, his arms, his chest, his back – everywhere her restless hands could reach.

Johnny Cash started to play – "Ring of Fire."

They were both breathing heavier when the kiss ended. She was surprised at a sudden looseness that told her he had unhooked her bra during their kiss. He brought the straps forward and pulled them down until the garment was removed and tossed to the floor. He moved back to study her.

His gaze was almost preternaturally intense in his aroused stated. His eyes drank in the sight of her exposed before him. His hands came up to cup her breasts as he accustomed himself to the weight and feel of them in his hands. He kneaded them and stroked the hardening tips with his thumbs.

She let her head fall back and her eyes slid shut in sheer hungry pleasure at his touch. He took advantage of the moment and began a sensual trail of slow kisses along her vulnerable throat to her mouth for a kiss that was wild and demanding.

He made a hungry sound deep in his throat and she shuddered with need. In that moment, she wanted him with a hungry desperation that scared her. She ran her hands along his sides and up his chest. When the kiss ended, she raised her head and looked up into his eyes as she pressed kisses to his chest. She nipped at his skin and tasted him with her tongue. She worked her way to his left nipple and nibbled and suckled until he groaned and ran his hands down her back to the waistband of the yoga pants she had slipped into earlier. He hooked his fingers into the waistband and pulled her pants and panties down with a swift moment until she shook them further down and stepped out of them.

AC/DC was now playing "Thunderstuck."

Again, he pulled back at arm's length just to study her in sequence – from her hair, her face, her bare breasts, her abdomen, her tiny waist and the robust flare of her hips and the triangle of honey-colored hair at the top of her thighs, to her long, shapely legs. He pulled her against him and the feel of his naked flesh against hers made her cry out with need. She reached for his belt and he helped her unbuckle it and unfasten his pants.

She helped him shuck the rest of his clothes and she took her turn to study him and she received a sensual shock.

An antiquated phrase suddenly came to her. She had always wondered what people meant by "hung like a horse." Now, she had an idea of what that meant. While, he was not freakishly porn-star large, he had the biggest erection that she had ever personally seen.

Her expression elicited a sexy chuckle from Clive. "Are you okay?"

She knew her eyes must have betrayed her thoughts. She looked pointedly at his penis. "I'm ... um ... intimidated ... What if it won't ... uh ... fit?"

He smiled at her – a little too wickedly for her peace of mind. "It will be fine. I promise."

He pulled her to him and the feel of their bodies together sent carnal shock waves through her. She felt like she was burning up from the inside out. He kissed her again and began to walk backward toward one of the chairs at the table. She was surprised. She thought they would end up on the bed. He sat down on the chair. His height brought his head almost exactly at the level of her breasts when seated. He slid his hands up over her breasts and caressed with such exquisite tenderness that she thought she would scream in frustration, but she suspected he knew exactly what he was doing to her.

"Bring me to Life" by Evanescence began to play.

He pulled her closer and leaned up to take one of her taut nipples into his mouth. He suckled and teased with his teeth and tongue until she was breathing as if she'd run a race. He moved to the other breast and repeated the same treatment. She wove her fingers into his hair and strained against his mouth. An insistent need had built to a raging inferno and her nether regions wept for release.

When he released her nipple, she pulled his hair to force his head back and she kissed him wildly – nearly mad with animal desire.

He used his legs to push her legs apart. He put his hands on her thighs and walked her up a couple of steps until she straddled the chair and his thighs. He reached between her legs and gently used the moisture that had accumulated there to moisten his fingers and he slide one finger between her nether lips until he found the hot spot that made her cry out in sheer sensual abandon. He slid two fingers inside her and used his thumb on the sensitive spot he used an alternating rhythmic motion that had her panting and brought her to climax within moments. Her head had fallen back during her orgasm and when it was finished she looked down to find him looking up at her with hungry eyes.

He did not say a word. He pulled her closer and worked the mechanics that helped her lower herself down until she was poised above the head of his erection. He positioned himself at her entrance and began to put pressure on her hips to lower her. She felt her body resist at first, but with his gradually increased pressure, her body finally stretched to accommodate him. She gasped in pleasure as she felt him slowly filling her. He pulled her downward until his body met hers where they were joined.

She was face to face with him now. She had never had a man so deeply encased within her. The pleasure was blindingly intense. They looked at each other – she saw a complex mix of emotions on his face. She also saw his upper lip was beaded with sweat as he fought to maintain control.

"My god, you are so tight ..." he murmured. "You were made to make me crazy, weren't you?"

She responded by licking the sweat from his lip and then kissing him deeply as he gripped her waist and began helping her set the rhythm as they rocked their bodies together. He moved his hips toward her as she raised up and rocked her hips down toward him. She did not expect to feel so much emotion. She was a fool to think she could complete this act without any feeling but lust.

"White Room" by Cream began to play.

She realized suddenly that she cared for Clive Clay. He had been her protector and her savior. He had been her companion and comforter and gradually her friend. He had become so much in such a short time. She did not have time to analyze her revelation as the rhythmic movement of their bodies built to a powerful climax.

He cried out and held tightly to her as he pumped his passion into her. His release sent her over the edge and she wrapped her arms around him and allowed her cries of pleasure join his.

Afterward, they came down slowly, holding on to each other, almost as if for dear life. He leaned back from her and brushed her hair back from her face. He cradled her face in his hands and used his thumbs to wipe away tears she didn't realize she shed. He kissed her again with such tenderness, she thought her heart would break.

Etta James' "A Sunday Kind of Love" began to play.

He wrapped his arms around her and stood. She hooked her legs around his waist and he carried her to the bed, their bodies still joined. He pulled back the covers and rolled onto the bed until she was on her back with him poised above her. He kissed her mouth and then worked his way down her throat. The game began until she felt him grow hard within her and they found their release again.

They fell asleep in each other's arms.

The music eventually stopped.

Shannon began to dream.

*****

Shannon stood in a bright and sunny conference room.

Naked.

There was a long conference table with leather office chairs - enough to seat at least 20 people with 10 on each side and possibly two more – one at each end. (The table was much like the one in the main conference room at the law firm where she worked). It was a very modern room with a row of floor-to-ceiling windows that banked the left side of the room and a white wall on the right and a very high ceiling with skylights.

The conference table was empty. The whole room was empty. She was alone.

She wandered to the windows and looked out. The room overlooked a vast, flat desert area. The land was rocky with hearty-looking plants, cacti, tumble weeds, and a Joshua tree here and there. There were mountains that sat like ominous thunderclouds on the distant horizon and closer to the right and left.

The sun, which sat high in the sky, spotlighted the closest and most prominent feature – a huge crater. The conference room appeared to be sitting along the crater's edge. From the side, the mouth of the crater had a bit of a rim that rose a good 30 feet from the desert floor, then the inside of the crater dropped at an incline so far down she would not hazard a guess as to the distance. She could clearly see the crater floor where some desert grass had managed to take root in patches. She noticed a long black line scarred the middle of the crater's floor as a crevice had opened. When seen from a distance, the crevice did not seem very large, but when she compared the crevice to the size of the crater, she realized the fissure was probably quite big if she were standing near it.

Something about the thought of standing near that crevice made her shudder.

Suddenly, she saw a reflection of a face in the glass. There was someone standing behind her! She gasped and whirled around.

Stanley stood before her.

"Oh, darling, what have you done?" he asked. He looked stricken.

She realized he was also naked ... and sporting an impressive erection.

"What do you mean? I don't understand."

He shook his head and slowly closed the distance between them. A quiet cough and the subtle shifting of movement drew her attention to the table, which was now nearly filled with people – men and women – all watching her intently with bright and hungry eyes.

They were all naked (at least from the waist up), but the men wore ties and the women wore pearl necklaces. It would have struck her as comical, except for the frightening intensity. Some of them wore wicked smiles and some licked their lips. Each person had a large, clear glass filled with cold water. She could see sweat running down the sides of the glasses. The people at the table did not appear to be thirsty.

With a firm hand, Stanley gripped her chin and forced her to look back at him. His familiar, silver eyes glittered preternaturally. "Don't worry about them. They won't move for fear of spilling the water."

"What does that mean? You're not making any sense." she whispered. She was not sure why, but she felt like she should.

"You're a smart girl. You'll figure it out. Your life will depend on it," he said and smiled in way that her Stanley would never have smiled.

A terrible dread crept over her – from the base of her spine to her scalp. She tried to back away from him, but he caught her around the waist and pulled her to him. He rubbed his erection against her. She felt the familiar stirring of her own arousal. She was shocked at her own reaction. Her body acted on its own accord. Her dread escalated to terror.

Stanley's smile was wickedly sensual. "Oh, no ... you don't get to run away, lover. Not after you worked so hard to get our attention. That was some powerful lust and guilt you were pumping out there. It was irresistible. Did you enjoy fucking the Fed? I think you did ... but can he do for you what I could? I don't think so ..."

She struggled against him as she felt an unnatural and powerful lust building. The feel of him against her felt so good – *too* good. She fought against her own body.

"I did it to stop you. I can't let anyone else die, Stanley," she said through gritted teeth.

An expression crossed his face and for a moment he looked like *her* Stanley again. He relaxed his grip enough to turn her around to face the window. He walked her to the window.

He whispered against her ear. He nipped at her earlobe and she shivered. "Did you enjoy the view? I made it especially for you."

"It's beautiful in a stark way. Where is it? What is it?" she asked.

He turned her around to slow dance with her. "*Ho-oh-me-ward bound ... I wish I was hoooomeward bound. Home, where my thought's escaping. Home, where my music's playing. Home, where my love lies waiting ... silently for me ....*" he sang.

She recognized the famous Simon and Garfunkel tune. "What are you saying?"

"I'm not saying anything, Sweetheart. You were smart enough to draw our attention ... then you will have to be smart enough to figure out the rest. Assuming you can survive ..."

She was utterly terrified now and almost desperately turned on. His body swaying against hers was driving her mad. He walked her backward toward the conference table. He only stopped when the table was pressed against her bare buttocks. The people at the table began to murmur excitedly.

"Stanley ... what are you doing? Please! This isn't you!"

She looked behind her and the glasses of water were gone. She knew this was not good. Suddenly, hands came to grip her arms and pull her up onto the table and forced her to lay down. The others had moved down to the end of the table. Hands were caressing her. Fondling her.

Stanley stood at the end. Her legs still dangled off and he summoned a few of the others to each take a leg. They bent her legs at the knees and then rolled them outward, essentially opening her fully for Stanley. He ran his fingertips along her thighs.

He looked into her eyes and winked, which she thought was odd. "If you want to survive, Shannon, then you will have to do something you've never been able to do before. You're going to have to resist me ... if you don't, you'll be mine ... you'll be *ours* if you give in. I'm getting too hungry to think straight anymore. Do you understand?"

She understood, but knew she was lost. She could feel the arousal throbbing in her nether regions. She was already moist. He slid his fingers into her and she cried out. Her back arched.

"Oh ... dear ... it looks like you're having trouble. It looks to me like you're enjoying this. You want this ... you know you do ..."

"No," she managed a hoarse whisper.

He removed his fingers and began planting kisses along her thigh as he moved his way toward the center of her universe at the moment. She wanted nothing more than what he wanted to give her. She fought hard to keep her sanity. She tried to struggle but the others held her in place.

He used his fingers to part her nether lips. He ran his tongue along the intimate seam. She cried out and her breath came in pants. "No ... please ... oh, god help me ... please .... Stop ... I don't want this ..."

He licked with a couple more strokes. She could feel an orgasm building. "No!" she screamed. Some primitive instinct told her if she climaxed, it was all over. She would be taken in by The Fog.

He paused for a moment and glanced up her body from his position at her *mons veneris* and looked into her eyes. "If you want to survive, you will have to do what you did last time and wake up. Just ... wake up, Shannon ..."

He licked another stroke and she moaned. "I don't know how to stop ... I don't know how to wake up!" she cried.

He lowered his head and she felt his tongue enter her. The orgasm was imminent and she struggled harder. He lifted his head and smiled at her ... and then he turned his head a little and bit a chunk out of her left thigh.

Her screams rivaled any horror flick she had ever seen.

*****

Clive awoke with a fierce need to take a piss. Shannon slept fitfully at his side. He gently untangled his limbs from hers, got up, and felt his way to the bathroom. He waited until he closed the door to turn on the light.

The light stung. He relieved himself and then stepped to the sink to wash his hands and splash water on his face. He stared into his own eyes in the mirror over the sink as the faucet ran. He looked at his haggard features as the water dripped down his cheeks in rivulets.

"What have you done, Clive?" he asked himself. Mama Clay's baby boy had been through a lot over the past year or so. He was in his late 30's, but he felt so much older now. His age was beginning to etch itself into the skin around his mouth and at the corners of his eyes. The markers of time and experience. He placed his hands on either side of the sink and leaned on his arms and dropped his head. He stood there for a few moments with his eyes closed.

He thought about his tryst with Shannon. Remembering the encounter caused him a strange mix of guilt and longing. The memory of her generous curves and passionate responses had an almost immediate effect on another part of his anatomy. He sighed and looked at himself again in the mirror. He couldn't quite meet his own eyes.

"You enjoyed it too much. You like her too much you son of a bitch," he accused his reflection.

A sound in the next room brought him immediately alert. He cocked his head to the side and listened. Shannon was murmuring and there was another low, eerie growling that made the hairs on the back of his neck try to crawl up toward the top of his head. He turned off the water so that he could hear better and he realized what the sound was.

Chester was growling.

He flung open the door -- throwing a shaft of light into the room. Chester was crouched under the table, which was across from the bed. There was a space below the motel room door and a gray/black churning cloud had slipped in ... was *still* flowing into the room. The line expanded into a large mass that took up nearly the entire end of the bed upon which Shannon slept.

The covers had been pulled down and she was being held down by several tentacles of fog and her legs were held wide open. There was a mass settled between her legs. A well-defined shadow-figure – male – worked between her legs and her back was arched. He could see her eyes were closed.

God only knew what she was dreaming.

"I don't know how to stop ... I don't know how to wake up!" she cried. Her straining limbs showed she was trying to fight the entity. The figure moving between Shannon's legs suddenly bit her thigh. Clive saw a visible portion was taken from her pale skin.

She screamed.

He looked on the table where he had left his weapon the night before. He knew that would do no good against this thing, so he grabbed the only other available weapon – the ice bucket. The ice had melted so he flung a good portion of water at the fog bank and then threw the ice bucket.

The moment the water hit the fog bank, a portion of it turned to a grainy-looking smoke and it dissolved and the rest of it formed into one large mass and hissed. It had pulled away from Shannon and he moved fast to snatch her off the bed. She was fully awake now and screaming. He clamped his hand over her mouth and pulled her backward into the bathroom – Chester zipped through the closing door just in time to miss having a heavy, commercial door slammed on him.

The fog had recovered enough to slam into the door. Shannon screamed behind his hand. He lowered her to the floor and she stood, shakily. Blood poured down her leg from the nasty wound.

The fog hit the bathroom door again and again. The door held.

He suddenly turned on the water and tried to get it to a comfortable temperature before the entity slammed against the door again. He flipped on the shower and grabbed Shannon around the waist and pulled her in with him. They wrapped their arms around each other and stood under the warm spray.

Chester stood on the floor and looked up at them with an "Oh, hell no!" expression.

The banging stopped. The doorknob began to twist back and forth.

Clive and Shannon held tighter to each other as they watched the door. Chester watched the door and then decided to jump in the shower with them when the door knob turned enough that the door began to open. The cat cowered at their feet and watched from around their legs.

The mass of fog rolled into the bathroom and created a dark wall – blocking out the light above the sink. Shannon trembled and whimpered. She buried her face in his chest.

"Remember me, motherfucker? You killed my wife! You're not getting anyone else. I'm coming for you!" Clive shouted at the mass. He was terrified and he was pissed.

A thick tentacle about the size of his waist reach out toward them. They shrank away from it. Clive reached up to the shower nozzle and turned to splash water at the fog. The tentacle dissolved and the larger mass hissed and drew back.

The fog drew back and waited. It waited until long past the time their fingers and toes turned pruny and long past the time when the water ran cold. He didn't think he could stand it much longer. Their only comfort was only what little body heat they could generate. Chester had moved to sit on their feet.

Finally, the entity pulled back into the bedroom area.

After several minutes, he stepped out of the tub, but motioned for Shannon to stay. She looked pitiful and nearly blue with cold. She wrapped her arms around her waist and shook, but nodded that she understood to stay put.

He crept forward as stealthily as his frozen limbs would allow. He moved into the main room, turning on lights as he went. He moved into the bedroom in time to see the last remnants of the fog bank slip out under the door. He grabbed a nearby towel rushed over to pack it into the space.

He grabbed two towels and threw one on the bathroom counter when he returned. He lifted Shannon out of the shower and began to vigorously dry her off. Her teeth chattered so violently for her to form words, but her dark eyes asked a question he understood.

"Yes, it's gone for now," he said. Her relief was heartbreaking.

He ran back into the bedroom and grabbed the comforter off the opposite bed and came back to wrap her in it and he led her back out to sit in one of the chairs by the table.

"H-h-h-h-how d-d-d-did you know about the w-w-w-water?" she managed to say between violent shudders.

"I didn't know," he answered. "I just grabbed the first thing I could use as a weapon."

She ran her eyes over him. "You n-n-n-need to p-p-put something on. Your f-f-f-e-e-eezing, too."

It tugged at his heart that, despite her pain and general misery, she was worried about him.

"Nah," he said. "Muscle generates heat. I have my big muscles to keep me warm." He bent his arm to display a bulging bicep. He was covered in goosebumps and obviously shaking from cold.

She managed a small semblance of a laugh.

Chester finally wandered out of the bathroom looking like a drowned rat. He stared at them both with a baleful glance. It was obvious he blamed them for the whole situation that involved him getting wet. Cats don't do wet. He shook off and threw water on them both, then skulked down under the table where he commenced the long process of grooming himself dry.

Ignoring the angry, wet cat, Clive pressed a glass of Scotch whiskey into her hand. "It helps with the cold ..."

She nodded and took a sip. Her shivering had slowed. "I think I know where's it's going ...I think Stanley was trying to tell me."

His heart lifted with that news. *Perhaps we will have a chance to survive this, after all.*

*****

Shannon's sucked in her breath sharply through her teeth as Clive cleaned her bite wound. She whimpered in pain. It was only about the size of a half dollar, but it was deep. At sunrise, he went and got his first aid kit out of the SUV. He cleaned and disinfected the wound and then bandaged it carefully.

"You really should get stitches. I can only do so much," Clive said. He looked up at her, his concern obvious.

"We don't have time." She got up and limped over to her suitcase to pull out some clothes. She began to get dressed. She was amazed that she still felt a little shy to be nude in front of him.

"Our experiment worked – Obviously. I think Stanley was trying to help us," she said as she pulled on a fresh pair of panties, taking care to stretch the leg opening so that it would not brush her wound.

"*Help us*?" His expression was incredulous. "He nearly killed you! He tried to *eat* you, Shannon. How's that helping us?"

She frowned as she put on a bra. She was too sore to get her arms around to the back to fasten it. He got up and came around the back to help her. She realized some of her sore muscles were his fault.

"I don't think he was trying eat me. I think he bit me to wake me up," she said. "He showed me some things in the dream. He kept giving me hints without alerting the Others that he was doing it. I don't think there's much left of the man I loved, but I think there is enough of him left to try to save us."

"We can talk about that later. First, you need to get some rest," he walked over to his first aid bag and pulled out a bottle. He opened it and tapped out a couple of pain pills. "You need to rest. It's daylight now. It does not have a history of attacking in daylight. So ... here take these and sleep while you can ..." He held his hand out to her.

"I will take those when we are on the road. I will sleep then. We need to get moving *now*. I don't think we have much time. They are going west ... Arizona, I think," she said. She related the crater and the scene Stanley showed her in the dream.

"Oh, shit! Shit, shit, shit! I think I know where that crater is," Clive said. He looked electrified as he rushed over to his file box. After shuffling through some papers, he pulled out a map. It was well worn from being folded and refolded dozens of times.

She saw that a circle had been marked in an area of Arizona, but it was inside a much larger red circle. "When I was initially investigating ...when the disappearances first started, I had figured that the killer must live within this radius because all of the disappearances were within this radius. This ..." he pointed to the area where the crater was located, "is inside that radius. It didn't make sense at the time because there is nothing there except desert and that crater. It is ringed with mountains."

"What do you mean?" she asked. Her injured thigh now throbbed ferociously.

"I mean we are going to hit the road. I think I know where this thing started and I think I know where we need to end it," he said.

She took a pain pill and packed her things as he packed his. They drugged Chester up – by now having learned of his status as a bad traveler – and put in him in his pet carrier and loaded up his supplies.

By the time they were loaded up and in the SUV, her pain pills had kicked in.

She heard Clive say, "All aboard for Arizona …" as he started the vehicle and then she drifted off to sleep.

*****

Clive knew a straight drive would be rough and he was right. The road trip was grueling. They took turns driving and sleeping – always carefully watching each other for signs of nightmares. They only stopped for gas, food, and bathroom breaks.

They arrived in Winslow in the early morning hours – around 24 hours later.

Shannon drove for the last four hours and it gave Clive ample time to think about a lot of things. They rode in near complete silence. It reminded him of the silence he experienced with comrades just before a raid – with each agent taking stock of their lives and coming to grips with the possibility he or she may not live to see another day.

He watched her profile. Each mile closer to their destination had carved deeper lines around her mouth. She had a warrior's look. She had changed so utterly from the woman he had met just a few days ago. *Had it even been a full week yet?* He did not have the energy to figure up the time. It didn't matter, really. They had been through enough together to share the same bond of two people who had spent years getting to know each other. She had proven herself to be kind, passionate, stronger than he had originally given her credit for, and incredibly brave.

Previously, it had been his professional duty to protect her. Now, it was also personal. He liked her. He respected her. Hell, given enough time, he was sure he could even love her, but he knew it was possible – even likely – that he would never get the chance to find out.

When they arrived, they found an older motel with a vacancy sign still on and checked in. It was actually more than just a generic motel – it had a romantic Spanish motif – and sported a nice courtyard. Once they had their bags in the room, Shannon made sure Chester was settled into the bathroom where he could use the litter box and have a meal.

He was waiting for her when she came out of the bathroom. He grabbed her and pinned her to the nearest wall, gripping her upper arms. They had not spoken to each other for nearly four hours. Their utter silence was solemn – funereal. He couldn't let things be this way while they had time left.

She gasped in surprise, but didn't fight. She trusted him.

He wanted her. He needed this and he hoped she did, too.

"Clive, I -," he stopped her words with his mouth. He kissed her slowly, but soundly. She responded with a fevered intensity. She began to unbutton his shirt and he did not have the patience for that, he pulled it and his tee-shirt off over his head.

He ripped her blouse open. Buttons popped off everywhere. He ripped the fabric. She murmured against his mouth, "You owe me a new blouse, G-man."

"Bill me," he said as he unfastened her jeans and moved her over to the standard motel room table. He unhooked her bra and pulled it off of her – kissing her all the while. He felt desperate, primitive, and out-of-control. He lifted her onto the table. It was small and her head hung back over the other side – her long hair dangling almost to the floor. He kneaded her breasts and suckled and nibbled until she cried out.

He yanked her jeans and panties down in one swift motion and pulled them off. He roughly pushed her legs apart – his only concession was to be careful of her wound. He wanted to taste her – to revel in her – to make her scream for him. He used his hands to spread her open for his viewing pleasure and then he used his lips and tongue to do what he set out to do- make her scream.

Once he had brought her to orgasm, he pulled her up and set her back on the floor. He looked into her dazed brown eyes as he unbuckled his trousers and pushed them down. He turned her around and bent her over the table and pushed into her from behind. The instant, liquid, silky heat of her sheathing him so tightly almost pushed him over the edge, so he remained still – throbbing inside her – until he felt he was in control enough to make it last. He began to thrust – slowly at first – and then with an increasing force and rhythm. He pushed deeper with each thrust until he felt the telltale signs that she had been pushed to the edge. She cried out and he let go – pumping his issue deep within her.

He braced his arms on either side of her as they both came back down and their breathing slowed. He gently pulled back out of her and helped her up and turned her around. She wrapped her arms around him and wept against his chest.

"I'm sorry if I hurt you or scared you …" he said as he stroked her hair and held her against him.

"You didn't hurt me. I … I just … needed that. It just made me a little emotional," she whispered. She sniffed wetly and laughed a little.

He smiled and kissed her hair. After a moment, she helped him get his trousers the rest of the way off and they got into the bed. They made love again as morning turned to noontime. This time, slowly and thoroughly … the way a pair of true lovers would do.

After a while, they lay in each other's arms and discussed their strategy for the dangerous reconnaissance mission ahead, which was very much *not* the way a pair of true lovers would do.

*****

Cheveyo and his companions arrived at the crater. They carefully rode their horses down the long and treacherous incline and set up camp just as the morning sun crested the top of the crater.

Pachu'a, easily the smallest of the five Shadow Warriors, looked around at the hundreds of dead crows decaying on the crater floor and made a whistling sound through his teeth. Wikvaya immediately began to remove the small black corpses so that there would not be any within a six foot perimeter of their campsite. He wore his hair pulled back in a long black braid which swayed from side to side as he worked.

Oaletaga moved forward and cautiously peered over the edge of the fissure. He used a flashlight to see how far down the crevice went, but returned to the others after a few minutes. He shook his head at Cheveyo. He was the oldest of the five which could be seen in the lines etched around his eyes and the strands of silver that had woven their way through his jet black hair.

"I could not see the bottom, Cheveyo," he said. He looked nervously back toward the fault. "I remember when it was just a scar on the crater floor. I had last visited it about two years ago. I think all of us have visited it many times when we were old enough. The evil was sealed up in the earth. That is what the Ancient Ones did for us – for the world – but I think it might have been an earthquake that re-opened it. I guess it doesn't matter now. The evil was released."

Cheveyo nodded. "That's what I think, too."

"When do you think the desert demon will come?" asked Hototo, abruptly. "*If* the desert demon comes."

"I think it will be tonight," he said. "The dreams told me what to look for. It will be tonight. The battle begins when the white man and woman come over the top of the crater," he said, pointing to the area where he had seen them in his dream.

Hototo was always a doubter, so Cheveyo didn't let it bother him. He knew – looking at Hototo's somber expression that his friend would do whatever was asked of him.

Pachu'a, Wikvaya, and Qaletaga were busy setting up the tent and the small campsite. They always did what they were asked. Hototo was the only one who questioned *everything*.

"When will we have to take the spirit potion?" Hototo asked.

Cheveyo went over to one of his saddlebags and unloaded a bag from which he pulled a decorated jug with a stopper, and he brought a special, ceremonial bowl, which had been wrapped in a blanket.

"We will drink it when we see the man and woman at the top of the crater, then we will go into the tent and drink ... and when the drink takes us ... then we will fight to kill the demon before it reaches the crevice. It hid there for many centuries and then rose again after the ground split open. We cannot let that happen again," Cheveyo said. "The elders from every tribe will be calling up the spirits to help us while we do this. They have already been working at this since dawn."

All five of the men turned to look at the crevice, which seemed darker and more sinister in the morning shadows.

It was going to be a long day of meditation and preparation for the battle.

*****

Shannon got up and showered while Clive went on his morning run. She let the water soothe her aches and pains ... and her fears. She had utilized a plastic bag and some duct tape to cover the bandage on her thigh wound, which throbbed with her every movement.

She acknowledged she was afraid – even terrified – of what lay ahead for them, but she had accepted the worst case scenario and was going to do whatever she had to do to accomplish her goal. She was going to find a way to destroy the Fog Bank.

After her shower, she fed Chester and petted him while he ate.

She was dressed and ready in jeans and a tee-shirt, with her hair pulled back in a pony-tail when Clive returned.

He eyed her apparel. "You'll need a jacket."

She looked at him doubtfully. "Are you sure? The temperature is going to get into the 90's today."

"You have no idea how cold it gets in the desert at night," he said. She noticed he had brought several bags with him. He put them on the bed and fished around in one of them until he brought out a shoe box. "You will also need these."

She took the box and opened it to find a pair of brown hiking boots. She nodded. It made sense.

"Thank you," she said as she sat down on the edge of the bed to lace up the boots before removing her tennis shoes and replacing them with boots. As she worked, she eyed the other bags. "What else did you get?

"I got weapons more suited to our enemy than my Glock," he said, patting the butt of the gun in his shoulder holster. He turned three bags over and a few dozen colorful variations on the same weapon tumbled onto the bed.

Her mouth fell open and she was completely speechless for several seconds. Finally, she looked at him – incredulous. "Water guns? We are searching for a man-eating fog monster with *water guns*?"

He scowled at her. "Don't look so shocked. You mark my words, sweetheart – these babies will save the day. Plus, these are not just *any* water guns. I got some great ones. I got some really good water pistols, but only as backup as they barely hold eight ounces of water. The best ones are the Super Soaker Scatterblast Blaster – which has a 22-ounce capacity and can hit targets up to about 30 feet away. I got several of those and a bunch of the pistols. We'll just have to use them carefully to try not to use up all the water at once."

She shook her head. "This is crazy."

"Yes, it is, but we have to have some way to defend ourselves if we run across that thing while we're in the crater. These should last until we can climb back up out of the crater and get to the SUV. These are not enough to destroy it, but I figure we can fight until we get to safety," he explained.

She felt better after she understood his logic. He bought an extra duffel to carry the water guns after they used the bathtub to fill them up.

It was late into the afternoon when they finally loaded up the SUV. She kissed Chester and nuzzled him. "We're leaving instructions in the room if we are not back by checkout time tomorrow, Chester. If something happens to us, then I just want you to know that I think you're the bravest cat in the whole world."

"*Meow*." Chester said. He nuzzled her for a moment and then wanted to be put down. Apparently, the cat was not big on sentimentality.

Clive had waited in the SUV while she wrote instructions for who to contact to take care of Chester and their belongings if their little adventure went horribly awry.

He smiled at her when she got into the vehicle. She was struck again at how handsome he was when he smiled. He smiled so rarely it was like a peek of sunlight on a stormy day.

"Was it an emotional good-bye? How did Chester take it?"

"Shut up," she said, wiping tears. Then, she laughed a little. "He is not as sentimental as I am."

Clive threw his head back and laughed. Shannon could not help but look at him and stare. She had never heard him emit a hearty laugh before.

She suddenly realized this whole situation energized him. She now understood why Ashley had said Clive had a second wife. He loved this kind of work.

"Come on, Sweetheart. Let's go find us a man-eating fog monster," he said, as they pulled out of the parking lot.

It was getting very late into the afternoon when they completed their journey to literally "the middle of nowhere." She had thought they were nearly there when they finally pulled off the main highway. She thought they were nearly there when they finally pulled off the graveled two-lane road onto a rutted service road and it was even longer before the rise that heralded the crater was in their sight.

Clive guided the SUV as close as he could until rocks and desert plants made it too risky to take the SUV any further. They would have to walk the rest of the distance before hiking up the side of the crater.

The sun had settled deeper toward its meeting with the horizon, but he assured her they would have enough daylight left to get to the bottom. They hiked about halfway up, sweaty and disgruntled by the extra difficulty of slipping around small, loose rocks and moving around large rocks, when they paused for a drink of water and for Shannon to catch her breath. She was in the midst of her breathless, sweaty misery when Clive tapped her shoulder and pointed into two different directions.

That is when she noticed they needed to step up their efforts.

A line of thunderclouds had formed to the North and East – not far from them.

A fog bank moved toward them from behind – from the South. It moved silently and swiftly along the ground.

They looked back at each other in horror. The fog bank was far, far larger than they had expected. She could clearly see Clive had a fear similar to her own mirrored in his icy eyes.

"It's too big for us to fight. We need to go," she said.

He looked back at the fog – it had progressed even closer and the storm continued to approach from an odd direction – if both threats approached at the same time, the storm would strategically flank the fog bank. The swiftly moving storm had already caused the wind to kick up.

Panicked, she asked, "Do we have time to make it back down to the SUV?"

He did a quick calculation. "No I don't think so. Let's finish this, Shannon."

She studied him for a long moment then, on impulse, she leaned forward and firmly kissed his mouth. She blinked back tears, but she was determined. "I'm with you. Let's do this."

They completed their climb much more quickly as they scrambled to the top. Looking down, they noticed a small campsite at the bottom of the crater.

Clive frowned. "What the hell?"

They did not have time to figure out who would be camping near such a large fissure. In the middle of a crater. In the desert. They ignored the oddity and began the long descent into the crater where they were certain the fog was headed.

*****

Ever vigilant, Wikvaya whistled for Cheveyo to come look when he spotted a white man and woman appear at the rim of the crater. He had been scouting the rim with a pair of binoculars for the last few hours. He handed the binoculars to Cheveyo. He saw the couple clearly. They paused. He could see the man pointing at his camp. They looked away after a moment and began their careful, decent to the crater floor.

He handed the binoculars back to Wikvaya. The older man and he shared a look. He could tell Wikvaya knew what he was about to say.

"We will to perform the drink ceremony, it is time. The man and woman are descending into the crater. The desert demon will not be far behind," he said.

Pachu'a, Qaletaga, and Hototo threw back the tent flap and gathered inside. Cheveyo hesitated as he felt the cool wind rising. He looked up and saw thunderheads beginning to move toward the edge of the crater. Wikvaya also looked up and then both men looked at each other. Cheveyo knew his own expression surely was similar to what he saw on Wikvaya's face now – a fierce pride.

"Our nation sent word for everyone who had the ability to do the ritual to entice the spirits to make rain – to do it. My grandfather made sure that they knew the Shadow Warriors needed their help. They have been at it all day," Cheveyo said.

Wikvaya looked back up. "If it continues to gather as swiftly and as powerfully as it looks now, then our people will have helped us destroy the desert demon. When the rain comes ...This will be a proud day."

They then joined the others in the tent. They all crowded in as close to a circle as they could get. Each had his own blanket. The tent provided some protection against the rising wind.

Once they were all settled, Cheveyo poured the spirit potion from the jug into an elaborately painted, ceremonial bowl.

Cheveyo raised the bowl and chanted in their native language – a warrior's prayer. When that was done, he said to his fellow warriors, "If I do not see you again in this life, I look forward to our reunion in the next."

He took the first drink, after which they passed the bowl around until all the liquid was gone.

One by one, each man fell over on his side as he succumbed to the effects of the spirit potion.

*****

Shannon noted the sky had gone dark -- the storm had almost moved completely over the mouth of the crater when she and Clive finally reached the floor. They were dirty and scratched and her thigh throbbed viciously.

They had both brought flashlights and, even though there was a little light left, they could no longer discern details because of the shadows. She shuddered at the first thing of significance she noted scattered all over the crater floor – hundreds of dead crows.

They walked what seemed like forever until they reached the fissure. Her impression from her dream was correct. The crevice that had opened up in the floor of the crater was very large. It ran most of the length of the crater – which was a good half mile across.

"It's so hard to believe this is an ancient disaster site. Ground zero. A meteor hit the Earth here with such impact that it left a permanent scar," Clive said quietly beside her.

She shined the beam of her flashlight down into the crevice as they approached. It looked like new earth shifted and fell within. She also noted some big rocks. Clive put out his hand to keep her from getting too close.

"The edges do not look stable and I cannot see the bottom. I'm not sure what opened it up. Maybe an earthquake ..." he said, but she was not sure if he were just thinking aloud or if he meant the information for her.

She did notice that one end of the fissure was wider than the other. Clive noticed it, too. "This is where we will set up. We will space ourselves about 10 feet apart. Each one of the water guns are supposed to be able to shoot to about 30 feet. We will place ourselves about halfway between the crevice – because I'm sure that's where it will be headed – and the crater wall."

She nodded and followed him about halfway. He figured the spot where he would make his stand and he dropped the black duffel he carried and pulled out about 10 water guns and five of the water pistols. He tucked four water pistols in the waistband of his trousers, with the butts sticking out, two in the back and two in the front of his waistband. He put the 10 water guns at his feet and lifted one to have it ready.

She lifted the duffel and walked away from him in a straight line until he shouted she had gone far enough. Her arm ached from the weight of the duffel after only 10 feet. She could not imagine how heavy it had been for Clive has he had carried it the entire way while it had been full. She dropped the duffel at her feet and took out four water pistols and tucked them into the waist of her jeans, the way she had seen Clive do. She positioned the water guns in easy reach and kept one ready to go in her hands.

The wind fairly howled around them now and lightning flashed. A peal of thunder shook the ground. From 10 feet away from her, Clive waved and then pointed. She looked and her heart began to pound and her limbs went weak at the sight of the massive fog bank rolling over the southern rim of the crater wall where they had just come down.

It moved smoothly and unnaturally against the wind. In fact, the wind did not seem to affect it at all. It was upon them in seconds – a wall of gray/black fog swirling toward them like a micro-tsunami.

Shannon did not wait, when it came within reach of the maximum distance of the water gun, she began to shoot. The Fog reacted violently – it shrank back with a metallic screech that rivaled the howling winds and the thunder.

She expected it would stop, but she did not expect that it would start throwing tentacles of fog – like a mutant octopus – toward her to try to disarm her. She shot water at everything that came near her. She assumed Clive was having similar trouble. Her first water gun emptied too soon. Whatever she hit would dissolve and the fog would screech and moan.

She found a savage satisfaction in the Fog Bank's cries of pain and loss. It occurred to her that she was going to set Stanley free of this thing or she would die trying.

The fog stopped – apparently considering a new strategy – and Shannon eyed it warily. She wanted to check on Clive but dared not look away from this thing for a second. The fog bank suddenly surged forward but divided and attempt to go around her. With part of it going to her left and part going to the right as it tried to get through the gap between her and Clive. She began to attempt to shoot in two directions at once.

Some of the fog bank managed to slip through and made its way toward the crevice. Shannon screamed, "No!"

However, there appeared to be a second line of defense.

Halfway between Shannon and Clive and the fissure line, were five native men. The tallest was easily eight feet and the others were close to that. Even the smallest of them was seven feet tall. Their eyes glowed yellow and they were dressed in full native regalia. All but one wore an elaborate, feathered headdress. The one without a headdress, wore only a beautiful, single hawk feather in his black hair. That one looked directly at her and smiled a terrifyingly fierce smile.

With a cry that made Shannon's blood run cold, the five warriors ran directly toward the Fog Bank and began tearing it to shreds with their bare hands. Tentacles of fog shot out and she finally recovered from her shock and began firing at any tentacles that came her way or would harm the warriors.

The warriors began to tear at the fog bank as if it were made of fabric – tearing it apart – rending it to shreds. The resulting screech nearly deafened her. The shreds were tossed aside, but she saw some of them begin to weave back together.

The smallest warrior fought the fiercest, but a tentacle of rent fog shot out and caught him around the neck and pulled ... and pulled ... until the warrior's head was ripped from his body. He turned to mist and disappeared. The four warriors left paused for a mere breath of a second and screamed then stepped up their tearing and ripping of the fog.

The storm had escalated to a whole new level with high winds whipping at her clothes, ground-shaking thunder, and cloud-to-ground lightning that sometimes came far too close for her comfort.

It was now full dark and she could no longer discern exactly where the fog was, so she just shot water in a perimeter around her. Her breath was terrified and ragged. She felt something tug at her left arm and looked down to see a dark tentacle wrapped around her upper arm – a dark strip around her gray jacket.

She screamed and dropped her water gun and grabbed one of the water pistols from her waistband and began firing water. Her arm began to burn like fire where the tentacle held her, but she kept hitting it with water until it dissolved and fell away.

Suddenly, a tentacle grabbed her around her left calf and yanked her leg out from under her. She screamed and landed hard on her back. The tentacle squeezed and pulled her toward a larger fog bank and she managed to scramble through the rocks and dead crows to grab her water gun and she began to fire at her leg. The tentacle had drawn her close enough that the fog created a deeper darkness all around her. Her screaming rose to panicked proportions and she fired wildly in all directions until suddenly another tentacle appeared and wrenched away the tentacle that had a death grip on her leg.

The rescuing tentacle wrapped around her arm and pulled her up to her feet. She was surrounded by darkness and she felt the tentacle brush her cheek and it suddenly occurred to her why this part of the fog had helped her.

"Stanley!" she cried. Her relief and grief nearly brought her to her knees again.

"Shannon ..." her name was spoken in a garbled, metallic-sounding whisper, "destroy us and set me free ... *destroy* us ... *please* ..."

Shannon's whole body shook with her sobs of grief. She raised her arms – water pistols in each hand – and began to fire into the fog where the voice had come from.

"I'm sorry," she cried on a choked whisper. "I love you … I love you …"

She fired wildly until the guns emptied and then she tossed them far from her and grabbed the next water gun in the duffel and a third pistol from her waistband. She fired until she watched several ripped areas of fog dissolve. It was hard to see in the darkness, but she knew that far too much of the fog remained. She wondered how Clive fared. She had heard him shout a few times, but nothing else.

She grabbed the duffel with the rest of the water guns and ran closer to the area where the warriors had first appeared – about halfway between her original position and the crevice. She looked over to see Clive had been pushed closer to the fissure.

Another warrior fell – tentacles had lashed around his arms and legs and he was ripped apart. His entrails and bits of flesh scattered but turned to mist and disappeared before hitting the ground.

The three remaining warriors continued to fight, but another one was torn apart so violently that Shannon screamed.

A tentacle shot out of the fog and hit Clive. He was knocked so far back that he fell and slid over the edge of the crevice.

"Noooooooooooo!!! Nooooooooo!!" Shannon screamed as she grabbed her duffel and ran to the edge. She could see his fingers, but knew he was barely hanging on. The edges were not stable.

"Clive!" she cried. She looked over the edge to see his face looking up at her – a pale oval framed by darkness.

"Shannon," his voice was rough with the strain of hanging on. She could see his body twisting as he struggled to find purchase to climb back up. She reached out to him. "No! Just keep fighting! You're not strong enough to pull me up if I can't manage it by myself."

She shook her head. "I'm not leaving you hanging here."

"Keep fighting, damn it! Keep it off me and out of this crevice. It can't go to ground, Shannon ... don't let it get in here ..."

His barked order made her jump up and grab another water gun from the duffel. She looked around. The fog bank had gained ground. A fourth warrior had fallen. There was only one left. It was the only warrior who had not worn a headdress.

It was down to her and him. She continued to fight until she was down to her last water gun but it emptied quickly and she and the big warrior were pushed closer to the edge of the crevice.

It was then that the skies opened up and released a torrent of cold, soaking rain.

The agonized screech of the fog bank was deafening and it began to shrink, but it still tried to lurch toward the crevice. The giant warrior turned and leaned down and yanked Clive up out of the crevice by his arm.

The agent (she had to admit to herself that at some point she had started to consider him her lover) immediately grabbed up his last water gun, which she had not seen laying nearby, and began to blast what was left of the fog bank.

Then ... all was quiet.

After several minutes of standing alert, they began to relax. She turned to thank the giant warrior, but he was gone. She turned back to Clive and began to walk toward him.

"We did it!" she shouted to him.

He was smiling and they met halfway. He grabbed her up and kissed her breathless. They held each other for a long time.

"You did a great job out there. You have good instincts. Did you ever think about joining The Bureau?"

She grinned. Ridiculously pleased with the compliment. They were both wet and trembling with cold. The rain had finally stopped.

He released her to begin gathering the water guns. "I think we need to grab our shit and go before we end up with pneumonia."

"You got it," she said. She moved to retrieve all the empty water guns. She had picked up the last one that she could see when she heard Clive shout.

She turned to see a single, thick tentacle of fog move up from the ground and it hit him in the chest. The scream that was torn from her came from so deep down that she did not even recognize it as her own voice. She began running toward Clive. He had fallen to the ground and the tentacle had wrapped itself around his arm and it was attempting to move toward the crevice and it was pulling Clive with it.

She grabbed Clive's legs, but could stop it. The thing was so strong. She began to pat herself down. She forgot she had one water pistol left. She began shooting the tentacle over and over until it dissolved and then she kept shooting it until the water ran out, screaming the whole time.

When she was sure it was all gone, she fell to her knees at Clive's side. He wasn't moving. She moved her flashlight over him. The tentacle had not just hit him in the chest, it had gone through him. There was blood pumping out of the hole.

She took off her jacket and used it to staunch the flow of blood. "Oh, no, no, no, no .... You do NOT get to die on me, Clive Clay!"

He looked at her. His icy blue eyes looked dazed, but he responded to her voice. "See? I told you those water guns would save the day." He gave a wet chortle that was supposed to pass for a laugh.

"No, Clive ... please don't leave me. Please ..." she begged. "Tell me what to do ... tell me and I'll do it."

He managed to raise one arm and he reached out to her. She took his hand. She could tell he could not see her clearly.

"Thank you, Shannon. Thank you for showing me how to live again," he whispered. He took a breath ... and then stopped breathing.

Shannon curled herself against his body and held him as she cried.

*****

Shannon was still by Clive's side shaking with cold when a Native American man came to her. He had two blankets. One to cover Clive and one to wrap around her. She sat up and studied him. As she gazed at him, she realized he was a normal-sized version of the giant warrior – the last survivor.

"How?" she asked. Her voice emitted as a croak from a throat raw with tears and cold.

"I am a shadow warrior, as were my five companions. I knew the desert demon had returned. I saw it in dreams, but I knew for certain when I came here and saw the ground had opened. I knew it had escaped," he said. "My name is Cheveyo and I am the only survivor of those who fought with me."

"My name is Shannon," she said. She looked down at Clive. The tears came again in hot abundance. "And, I am the only survivor, as well."

"Shannon, you need to come with me. I will get you out of here and we will get help to retrieve our friends."

She allowed him to pull her to her feet. Nearby, she saw a single, beautiful hawk feather. The one Cheveyo had worn in his hair when he was the shadow warrior. She walked over and retrieved it. She tried to hand him the feather, but he refused.

"No, keep it. You found it, the spirits meant for you to have it. It will serve as a reminder of your bravery and the sacrifices of those who fought with you," he said.

Shannon cried as she tucked it into her waistband and covered it carefully with her tee-shirt.

Cheveyo climbed up on his horse, then handed her up to sit in front of him. It was time to climb out of the crater and go home.

The battle was done.

*****

One Year Later

Shannon kissed her baby boy and laid him in his bed for the night. The sun was setting and she loved this time of day. The windows in the nursery were perfect to watch the sunset. She liked her new apartment. She started over when she returned. She moved to a smaller town where she could work and begin college – pre-law.

Her son was an unanticipated part of her plans, but she could not imagine her life without him. She fed him, and then rocked him as she sang the Black Crows' "Hard to Handle" to him softly. He fell sound asleep.

She had a paternity test done early on, but it only confirmed what she already knew. Her little man was a miniature Clive Clay, but with Shannon's brown eyes. His focus and intensity was comical in an infant. She loved the way he studied everything in his most alert moments. He particularly loved his mobile. She had made it herself.

She studied the mobile now with its tiny hawks soaring in a circle over his bed. A beautiful hawk feather hung in the center of the mobile.

She sighed and knew she had to tear herself away. She had studying to do.

"Chester …" she called quietly. The large gray cat appeared immediately and curled up under the baby's crib. Her cat was a great watchdog. She knew he would alert her if there was any trouble.

Not that she expected any.

As part of her nightly ritual, she always whispered from the doorway – a prayer for both him and for herself.
"I wish you the sweetest of dreams."

The End

ACKNOWLEDGEMENTS

Cover art by: © Chalermphon Kumchai | Dreamstime.com - <u>Silhouette of action of woman scream</u>

The cover design was by Leigh McQueen.

The author would also like to thank her friends and family for their constant support and encouragement – and Facebook stalking – to keep her moving to complete the Fog Bank Trilogy. It kept me going on those nights when I was too tired to write – but I did it anyway. I didn't want to let you down. I hope the ending was worth the waiting.

Finally, I took liberties with geography and with an interesting mix of fictional town names and real ones, so don't think I lost my mind … ;D … I actually did that on purpose.

The original story began in the spring of 2015 with a little "vision" I had of a man hiding in the fog … he was part of the fog and he had his sights set on a young woman. Once I completed the third one, I have worked hard to sell each novella, always with the intention that I would put them all together in one volume – and now here it is. I hope you enjoyed it. If you did … leave me a review. I'll love you forever for it!

COMING SOON
Halloween 2016
The Witch of Hadler's Woods
A novel by Leigh McQueen

Jeremy Fowler is a freak, but it's a secret – a secret he is having a hard time keeping. He has had an "imaginary" friend named "Kinal" since he was five years old. The problem is that he is almost 23 and his imaginary friend still exists and has grown demanding. Fearing for his sanity, and at Kinal's insistence, Jeremy decides to spend the summer after graduation in his hometown of Cummings, Tennessee. Kinal's demands grow more urgent and Jeremy finds himself drawn to the thick woods on the North side of town – a hundred acres owned and protected as a historical site. Known as Hadler's Woods, it has been the source of fear, fascination, and superstition for generations. It is said that there is a witch who lives deep in Hadler's Woods and Kinal is insisting that Jeremy go and meet her.

For what purpose? Unfortunately, Kinal is keeping that to himself.

Made in the USA
Charleston, SC
05 March 2017